# FRENCH CHANSONS FOR THREE VOICES (ca. 1550)

## Part I:
## Three-Part Chansons Printed by Gardane (1541$^{13}$)

RECENT RESEARCHES IN THE MUSIC OF THE RENAISSANCE

*James Haar and Howard Mayer Brown, general editors*

---

A-R Editions, Inc., publishes six quarterly series—

*Recent Researches in the Music of the Middle Ages and Early Renaissance,*
Margaret Bent, general editor;

*Recent Researches in the Music of the Renaissance,*
James Haar and Howard Mayer Brown, general editors;

*Recent Researches in the Music of the Baroque Era,*
Robert L. Marshall, general editor;

*Recent Researches in the Music of the Classical Era,*
Eugene K. Wolf, general editor;

*Recent Researches in the Music of the Nineteenth and Early Twentieth Centuries,*
Jerald C. Graue, general editor;

*Recent Researches in American Music,*
H. Wiley Hitchcock, general editor—

which make public music that is being brought to light
in the course of current musicological research.

Each volume in the *Recent Researches* is devoted
to works by a single composer or to a single genre of composition,
chosen because of its potential interest to scholars and performers,
and prepared for publication according to the standards that govern
the making of all reliable historical editions.

Subscribers to this series, as well as patrons of subscribing institutions,
are invited to apply for information about the "Copyright-Sharing Policy"
of A-R Editions, Inc., under which the contents of this volume
may be reproduced free of charge for study or performance.

Correspondence should be addressed:

A-R EDITIONS, INC.
315 West Gorham Street
Madison, Wisconsin 53703

RECENT RESEARCHES IN THE MUSIC OF THE RENAISSANCE • VOLUME XXXVI

# FRENCH CHANSONS FOR THREE VOICES (ca. 1550)

## Part I: Three-Part Chansons Printed by Gardane (1541[13])

Edited by Courtney S. Adams

A-R EDITIONS, INC. • MADISON

ISSN 0486-123X

ISBN 0-89579-155-2 (v. 1)
ISBN 0-89579-156-0 (v. 2)

Library of Congress Cataloging in Publication Data:

The French chanson à 3 ca. 1550.

(Recent researches in the music of the Renaissance , v. 36-37 ISSN 0486-123X)
For cantus, tenor, and bassus.
1. Chansons, Polyphonic. I. Adams, Courtney. II. Gardano, Antonio, 1509-1569. III. Adrian, LeRoy & Robert Ballard (Firm) IV. Series.
M2.R2384 vol. 36-37 [M1529.4] 81-14927
ISBN 0-89579-155-2 (v. 1) AACR2
ISBN 0-89579-156-0 (v. 2)

# Contents

Part I

## Part II



### Three-Part Chansons Printed by Gardane ($1543^{21}$)



### The *Tiers livre de chansons* Printed by Le Roy and Ballard ($1553^{22}$)

# Preface

## General Remarks

During the sixteenth century, chansons appeared in large numbers and in diverse forms. The pieces in the three source-anthologies selected for this edition illustrate the wide variety of styles present in the three-part French chanson from the early years of the century to 1553. Although two of these sources were published in Venice (in 1541 and 1543), their editor was Antoine Gardane, a Frenchman newly arrived in Italy. A composer as well as an editor, he no doubt had close contact with French musical taste. The third source-volume, issued by Le Roy and Ballard in Paris, appeared in 1553, shortly after the firm began its publishing operations. All of the chansons from Gardane's large anthology of 1541, together with their texts, translations, and critical apparatus, are presented in Part I of this edition. Part II presents chansons, texts, translations, and critical apparatus for the three-part works from Gardane's later print of 1543 and from the *Tiers livre de chansons* printed by Le Roy and Ballard. This preface discusses all of the music in both parts of the edition and appears only in the present volume. In the Preface, the chansons of Part II are identified both by number and by source-printer to make clear which of the two anthologies is indicated (for example, "Part II, no. 1 Gardane" or "Part II, no. 1 LRB"). The contents of these three prints from the mid-century reflect all the major stylistic trends found in the three-part chanson during the first half of the century.

The first fifty years of the sixteenth century were of particular significance in the development of the chanson. Toward the beginning of this period, composers lost interest in three-part writing and turned instead to a four-voice medium. In addition, many writers adopted a new chordal texture that came to be known as "Parisian" style. Recent research has shown that the "Parisian" chanson for four parts was a far more complex phenomenon than one all-encompassing term would suggest.[1] Such is the case for the three-voice chanson as well, as the contents of this edition will show.

A few of the compositions in these three prints originated as early as the first decade of the century; others were probably written closer to 1550. In general, the later works differ from the earlier ones in the following ways: (1) the newer works have a closer relationship of word to music (text underlay is less problematic); (2) they make use of exact musical repetition as opposed to varied repetition; (3) they use shorter phrases and have a shorter overall length; (4) they have a more pronounced rhythmic pulse; (5) there is a reduction of melismas in favor of declamatory style; and (6) there is a clearer sense of tonality that is particularly noticeable at cadences. A comparison of an "early" chanson like Févin's "Fors seullement la mort" (Part II, no. 11 LRB), composed before 1512, with a "late" chanson such as one of the works in this edition by Claudin de Sermisy or Jacques Arcadelt illustrates these differences.

The choice of vocal ranges in these chansons can be used as a general guide in dating the composition of the works. A composer writing for three voices had four ranges from which to select, and fashion shifted over the fifty-year period represented by the chansons in this edition. In chansons composed in the early part of the century, a bass range is common for the third voice (see Part II, no. 8 LRB), but by 1550 the bottom part had risen from the bass register to that of a tenor and sometimes even to that of an alto (see Part II, no. 4 LRB). The relationship between the two upper parts was also subject to change. Among the early chansons, the upper voices are often low (sometimes in the tenor range), with some crossing of parts (as in Part I, no. 1). Chansons composed later, such as some of those published by Attaingnant in 1535, employ two truly equal superius voices in the soprano register (see Part I, no. 23). Other chansons, which appear in publications of 1535 and earlier, keep the upper lines separate and contain occasional passages of parallel writing at the interval of a sixth (as in Part I, no. 8).

Textures could be totally homophonic or totally contrapuntal, but most settings are comprised of a mixture of these elements. Many chanson composers, in fact, pursued a middle course by using homorhythmic passages that, while permitting imitative entries, have a chordal impact (see Part II, no. 13 Gardane).

Borrowing of melodic material occurred frequently in three-part writing. Early in the century the sources for this borrowing were often popular tunes; the borrowed melody was placed in the tenor, where it was set apart by rests and longer note values (see Part II, no. 6 Gardane). Later, the chanson composers drew on both popular and courtly models, and the melody appears more commonly in the superius (as in Part I, no. 8).

Seven of the chansons in this edition appear in more than one of the source-anthologies. To avoid duplication in such cases, only the version given in the earlier source has been included in the music portion of the edition. The title of the concordant piece, however, retains its proper position in the Contents and Critical Commentary for the later source-anthologies, and the reader is given a cross-reference.

Attributions to specific composers, sometimes conflicting ones, are given in the concordances for all but eleven chansons in the present edition. However, less than one-quarter of the poems set in the chansons of this edition can be attributed to an author; these texts are the work of Clément Marot, Mellin de Saint-Gelais, and perhaps Claude Chappuys, all well-known poets. Anonymous texts are typical of chanson poetry written prior to 1525, so the large proportion of unknown authors is not surprising. Only gradually, as such poetry became more fashionable, did poets' names become associated with the texts.

Clément Marot is significant in this literary development—he refined the rather rough verse of many of his anonymous contemporaries and offered a variety of forms for the composer to set. Although his chanson poems are frequently courtly expressions of unrequited love, occasionally his poetry also reflects folk influence (see Part I, no. 30). Perhaps Marot's greatest skill was his ability to bridge these two traditions. The presence of numerous chansons by Claudin de Sermisy in the source-anthologies explains the predominance of Marot's poetry relative to that of the other poets represented here. Claudin's preference for Marot's texts was of long standing, going back to the time when they were both associated with the French court of François I.

Claude Chappuys and Mellin de Saint-Gelais were also connected with the court of François I, a patron of the arts who was himself a poet. Chappuys was noted for his verse in both French and Latin, although his reputation never quite equaled that of his contemporaries Clément Marot and Saint-Gelais. Arcadelt had a special preference for Saint-Gelais's writing,[2] and in some instances Saint-Gelais's poems were published as chansons even before they were printed as poetry.

In general, chanson collections from early in the century employ short poems (often only four or five lines). Longer poetry is characteristic of collections published just before 1550,[3] and the inclusion of more than one verse of a poem is rare in chanson prints issued before 1550. The three source-anthologies for the present edition confirm this progression. The texts of works known to originate before 1520 all contain only four or five lines (see Part I, no. 16; Part II, nos. 11 and 19 LRB). The later poems by Marot are generally longer (see especially Part I, nos. 5, 15, 27, and 30), and added verses appear only in the third and latest print, of 1553 (Part II, nos. 14, 15, 16, and 25 LRB).

The chansons of the present edition can be performed either vocally (with one voice to a part) or instrumentally. A combination whereby one or sometimes two of the upper parts are sung and the remaining line or lines are played is also appropriate. Sixteenth-century performance practice varied, depending upon the availability of singers and instruments, and many prints advertised their suitability for either vocal or instrumental interpretation. Although many of the texts express the sad sentiments of unrequited love and other misfortunes, performers should not be persuaded by the texts to select too slow a tempo. In many cases, the unhappiness of the poem is belied by the character of the music, which suggests a more lively interpretation.

## The Three-Part Chansons Printed by Gardane ($1541^{13}$): *Di Constantio Festa . . . trenta canzoni francese di Janequin*

### *The Anthology*

Although he was born in France, Antoine Gardane (1509-1569) spent a large portion of his life in Italy and finally changed his name to Antonio Gardano in 1555. His publications were perhaps the first in Venice to employ the single-impression technique with movable type that Attaingnant had initiated in Paris. A man of many interests, Gardane also printed some non-musical books and was active as a composer.[4] His editions, the first of which appeared in 1538, specialize in the madrigal. Gardane also issued a few volumes of chansons in the early years of his publishing career, but his interest in this genre was apparently of limited scope. Although, from time to time, he produced reprints and slightly altered editions containing chansons, these later volumes are comprised essentially of pieces from the six basic collections that he had published between 1538 and 1543.[5]

Part I of this edition reproduces the chansons of Gardane's print of 1541, in which thirty chansons follow forty-two madrigals. This print has achieved considerable notoriety in musicological literature due to the misleading nature of the title. Gardane advertised the book as a collection containing three-voice madrigals by Costanzo Festa, forty madrigals by Gero, and thirty chansons of Janequin. In fact, the print includes only one madrigal by Festa (unidentified in the book), one madrigal of Parabosco, and forty madrigals by Gero. Of the thirty chansons supposedly by Janequin, twenty-one have been shown to be by other composers, and there is no reason to view any of the remaining nine as the work of Janequin. Presumably, Gardane used the names of Festa and Janequin in the title of his 1541 anthology to increase the sale of the volume.[6]

Another factor, however, may also have contributed to Gardane's attempt to mislead his public. His ten-year printing privilege in Venice required that his publications contain new works never before printed, that they be issued in Venice at the rate of at least one folio a day, and that they be published on paper of reasonably good quality.[7] However, twenty-four of the thirty chansons Gardane included in his print of 1541 can be traced to earlier sources, and in all likelihood the other six pieces were also "borrowed" from available prints. Thus, Gardane may well have believed that attributing the chansons to Janequin had the advantage of obscuring their origins in previously existing prints.

Gardane issued this 1541 collection as a set of three partbooks (cantus, tenor, and bassus). Of particular interest is his method of organizing the chansons within the print. Although the pieces are in various modes, all of the first seventeen works contain a B-flat in the signature; the remaining thirteen pieces lack signature accidentals. Rather than group the chansons by mode (the more usual system), Gardane chose to divide them according to whether or not their modes were transposed.

Another unusual aspect of the print concerns the low ranges of the works. Over half of the pieces in Gardane's 1541 edition have been transposed down a fourth or a fifth, relative to their pitch-levels in most other concordant prints or manuscripts (see the Critical Commentary). The few other editions from this period that also use low pitches for these chansons clearly have a print by Gardane as their source, since they also duplicate the misattribution to Janequin. Eight chansons appear in the 1541 edition at the lower fifth with a flat added (Part I, nos. 2, 3, 4, 5, 6, 11, 13, and 15); and in eight other pieces, Gardane has removed the flat and transposed them down a fourth (Part I, nos. 18, 22, 23, 25, 26, 27, 29, and 30). As a result, the superius part in the 1541 collection never exceeds d'', a pitch within the reach of a countertenor. Although pitch notation should be viewed as relative rather than absolute at this time, Gardane had a clear predilection for the low register. Perhaps he simply preferred low ranges, or, more likely, he wanted the pieces notated so they could be sung by males only, if necessary. In the present edition, these chansons are transcribed at their higher pitches; Gardane's transpositions can be determined from the musical incipits given at the beginning of each chanson, or from the citations given in the Critical Commentary.

The title of the print indicates that the publication of 1541 is a corrected version of an earlier edition, one that is now lost; and further evidence suggests the existence of such a prior collection. In 1540, the German publisher Kriesstein issued a book containing "Je ne fais rien que requérir," one of the pieces published by Gardane in 1541 (see Part I, no. 4). In Kriesstein's print, the chanson appears at Gardane's low transposition, together with a misattribution to Janequin. Thus, Kriesstein must have taken the chanson from a print by Gardane—in all probability the earlier version of Gardane's 1541 edition.

A revision of the 1541 version appeared later ($1543^{23}$), with some alterations affecting both the cadential elaboration and the order in which the thirty chansons were presented. (There is no longer quite so rigorous a grouping according to signature accidentals.) With regard to the cadences, Gardane, a composer as well as an editor, could not resist the opportunity to add his own improvements to this 1543 revision. Curiously, his changes are not consistent. In some instances the cadences are simplified; in others, they are made more ornate. Neither the 1541 nor the 1543 print employs ligatures, although ligatures do occur in many of the concordances and in later publications of Gardane's. The fact is that his font contained no ligatures until 1545.[8]

*The Music and Composers*

A single source—the *Trente et une chansons musicales a troys parties* issued by Attaingnant in Paris in 1535—contains concordances for eighteen of

Gardane's thirty chansons and attributions for sixteen pieces.[9] Although only one partbook from Attaingnant's print is extant, its designation "Primus Superius" suggests that most of these three-voice works were conceived for two superius parts and one lower voice.

Of the pieces attributed to specific composers by Attaingnant, most are ascribed to Claudin de Sermisy, a leading musician of the day.[10] Claudin's chansons *à 4* (published in large quantity beginning in 1528) are considered models of the new "Parisian" chordal style for four voices. However, the homophonic texture associated with many of his four-part chansons does not appear in any of his three-part works. Instead, the phrases open with imitation, almost always in two voices and occasionally in three. The eleven chansons *à 3* by Claudin that appear in Gardane's 1541 anthology (nos. 3, 4, 5, 6, 11, 13, 18, 22, 23, 27, and 30 of Part I) are unified in several other respects. They all contain an exact musical repetition of one or more phrases, generally at the beginning or close of the work. Most of them employ considerable crossing of the two upper parts; in fact, two works, "Au pres de vous" and "Contre raison" (Part I, nos. 6 and 11), have been written for three equal voices with continuous interchanging of parts. In addition, these eleven pieces all represent Claudin's arrangements of four-voice chansons that were, in most cases, also composed by him. Sometimes in these adaptations a single part is borrowed almost exactly and placed in either the tenor or the superius of the three-part version. In other instances the borrowing is partial or may shift from voice to voice. Most of the texts set by Claudin in Gardane's 1541 publication deal with love, a primary poetic concern of the period, and five of the poems set by this composer can be attributed to two poets: Clément Marot (Part I, nos. 4, 5, 27, and 30) and Claude Chappuys (Part I, no. 13).

The style of Guillaume Le Heurteur, who is represented by three chansons (Part I, nos. 2, 14, and 17) in Gardane's collection, differs from that of Claudin. Although Le Heurteur's works also derive from four-part chansons, the borrowed melody is stated freely in all three voices. As a result, all the parts participate regularly in the imitation, and the lowest voice is generally more melodically conceived than that in Claudin's chansons. Two of Le Heurteur's pieces (Part I, nos. 2 and 17) use declamatory style in fast eighth-note passages, unlike Claudin's three-part chansons, which generally employ melismas for eighth-note sections. Because Le Heurteur's only known association was with the church of Saint-Martin in Tours, he was probably a provincial rather than a Parisian composer.[11]

Among the oldest chansons in the 1541 print are "Hellas, je suis marry" and "C'est donc pour moy" (Part I, nos. 16 and 28). The former was composed by Antoine de Févin (d. 1512), and the latter, which has conflicting attributions to Ninot le Petit and Willaert,[12] first appeared in a manuscript that could not have been compiled after 1509.[13] Neither piece relates to any four-part model, and they both lack the clear rhythmic and tonal profile of the newer works in Gardane's collection.

Cosson's chanson, "Mauldicte soit" (Part I, no. 9) provides a marked contrast to this older style. Written for two rival upper parts, this piece is one of the fashionable reductions from a four-voice original favored by Claudin and Le Heurteur (the tenor contains an exact duplication of the borrowed melody). Based on a text by Marot, this composition was first published in 1539 by Moderne, a printer with a reputation of preferring newly composed pieces.[14] Only three chansons by Cosson are known, and two of them appear in this edition (Part I, no. 9 and Part II, no. 5 Gardane).

The nine pieces by anonymous composers in Gardane's 1541 print (nos. 1, 7, 8, 10, 12, 19, 20, 21, and 24) show a wide stylistic diversity, as the following discussion of three of these chansons will demonstrate. "Le cueur de vous" (Part I, no. 12) resembles a typical three-part courtly chanson by Claudin. Based on a poem by his favorite poet, Marot, the chanson represents a reduction of a four-voice work by Claudin, with the superius duplicated exactly. At the opposite end of the spectrum is "Jennette, Marion" (Part I, no. 1) with its bawdy text, declamatory refrain, and simple repetitive harmonies. "Amour, Amour, tu es par trop cruelle" (Part I, no. 8) is the most homophonic work in the collection. It resembles a number of three-part pieces published by Attaingnant (in his *Quarante et deux chansons* of 1529) just as the so-called "Parisian" style, with its emphasis on clear-cut phrases and chordal textures, was emerging. This short piece is divided syllabically and musically after the first four syllables. Cadences are clearly delineated, and the final phrase is repeated. Some parallel writing at the sixth takes place between superius and tenor, there is no crossing of parts, and the lowest voice maintains a true bass ambitus.

The two works attributed by Attaingnant to Gosse, "Amour, me voyant" (Part I, no. 15) and "Si j'ay eu" (Part I, no. 29), are both adaptations of four-part chansons by Claudin de Sermisy. In the former piece, the superius of the model appears quite exactly in the upper part of the three-voice setting; in the latter work (with a conflicting attribution to Ysoré by Gardane), the superius of the four-part version is duplicated in the tenor. The three-part writing of Gosse and Ysoré is too similar to resolve this conflict of attribution on stylistic grounds.

Gascongne's two chansons (Part I, nos. 25 and 26) appear to have been well-liked, since they were reprinted by Le Roy and Ballard as late as 1578 in a set of retrospective collections that specialized in successful chansons from the mid-century and earlier. Both works are based on texts of a popular nature and have the imitative settings that are typical of Gascongne. Although some concordances ascribe "Je suis trop jeunette" (Part I, no. 26) to Gombert, bibliographic and stylistic considerations support the attribution to Gascongne (see the Critical Commentary).

In general, among the chansons of Gardane's 1541 collection, the rules of good voice leading do not seem to have been of primary concern to the composers. Parallel fifths are not uncommon (even in the works of reputable composers), and melodic leaps of a ninth and passages of exposed parallel fourths also appear on occasion.

## The Three-Part Chansons Printed by Gardane ($1543^{21}$): *Primo libro di madrigali d'Archadelt a tre voci*

### *The Anthology*

Soon after the appearance of the 1541 edition, Gardane issued two almost identical prints containing, in addition to madrigals and motets, more three-part chansons ($1542^{18}$ and $1543^{21}$). In spite of the similarity of the contents of these later publications (see Sources and Editorial Methods for details), the more complete second version ($1543^{21}$) was chosen for transcription here. This second print includes an additional chanson, although the reprinted title *(Primo libro di madrigali d' Archadelt a tre voci con la gionta di dodese canzoni franzese et sei motteti novissimi a tre voci)* continues to refer to twelve rather than thirteen chansons.

The 1543 print appeared in the same format as Gardane's 1541 publication (three partbooks, entitled cantus, tenor, and bassus), but Gardane no longer showed as much concern for low ranges. A top note of g'' is not uncommon in the superius; and the chanson "Si j'ay eu" (Part II, no. 9 Gardane) that was given a low transposition in the 1541 edition reappears transposed up a fourth in Gardane's books of 1542 and 1543. Although the madrigals and motets of this 1543 print mix transposed with untransposed modes, the chansons are treated consistently—all thirteen have a B-flat in the signature.

### *The Music and Composers*

In addition to being the main source of concordances for Gardane's 1541 print, Attaingnant's *Trente et une chansons* (see above) is also a basic source for Gardane's 1543 anthology. The *Trente et une chansons* and Gardane's 1543 print have six chansons in common; but there is a curious discrepancy of attributions between Attaingnant's source and Gardane's publication for all six of these pieces. Four anonymous chansons from Attaingnant's print appear with attributions to Claudin in Gardane's book (Part II, nos. 2, 3, 7, and 13 Gardane), and two chansons ascribed to Gosse by Attaingnant are assigned by Gardane to Ysoré and Jacotin (Part II, nos. 9 and 11 Gardane). Although these may be bona fide corrections on Gardane's part, the cavalier attitude he showed toward attributions in the 1541 print gives rise to some uneasiness about his accuracy here. In the case of three of the chansons (Part II, nos. 2, 3, and 13 Gardane), Gardane appears to be the first editor to ascribe them to Claudin. However, if they were indeed by Claudin, one wonders why Attaingnant, who was closely associated with Claudin, didn't make these attributions to Claudin, along with his other eleven ascriptions, when these pieces were published earlier, in 1535.

Stylistically, however, there is no reason to question Gardane's attributions to Claudin. All four of the chansons attributed to Claudin in Gardane's 1543 print (Part II, nos. 2, 3, 7, and 13 Gardane) are similar to Claudin's three-part style as described above, and two of the texts are by Marot (see nos. 2 and 13). "Il est en vous" (Part II, no. 7 Gardane) is another example of a work by Claudin that was composed for the unusual combination of three superius parts.

Of particular interest in this 1543 collection is the piece by François du Boys, "J'ayme bien mon amy" (Part II, no. 6 Gardane), which is based on a monophonic chanson.[15] Du Boys's setting is a perfect illustration of a *chanson rustique*, a genre popular around 1515 and earlier.[16] In these chansons, the borrowed melody (often simple and repetitive) is placed in the tenor and separated from the other parts by the use of longer note values and rests between entrances. Usually the tenor voice is the last to begin each phrase. The vocal ranges are low and in close proximity to one another; in fact, the bottom voice sings above the superius on occasion.

Other chansons that contain elements of this style include Févin's "Hellas, je suis marry" (Part I, no. 16), two chansons by Gascongne (Part I, nos. 25 and 26) from Gardane's 1541 print, and the anonymous "J'ay mis mon cueur" (Part II, no. 12 Gardane) from his 1543 collection. This setting of "J'ay mis mon cueur," which uses a popular monophonic chanson in the tenor, should not be confused with the three other versions *à 3* of the same text and melody.[17]

The piece by Certon included in Gardane's 1543 publication is unique, since it represents the only three-part chanson known to be written by this successful Parisian composer (Part II, no. 1 Gardane). Certon borrowed not only the text, but also most of the melody and portions of the harmony from an earlier setting for four voices by Janequin. The short phrases, tuneful melody, simple harmonies and declamatory refrain reinforce the popular character of the text.

Cosson's "Voyant souffrir" (Part II, no. 5 Gardane), like his "Mauldicte soit," has two equal upper parts and uses a borrowed melody; the remaining works in the print (Part II, nos. 4 and 8-11 Gardane) reflect the same reliance upon four-voice models that characterized the newer works in Gardane's 1541 collection.[18] Two of these chansons (Part II, nos. 8 and 10 Gardane) have equal upper parts, whereas the others (Part II, nos. 4, 9, and 11 Gardane) maintain different ranges for the top voices. In sum, then, the print of 1543, like that of 1541, contains works from varying style periods—the two pieces in an older style (Part II, nos. 6 and 12 Gardane) are based on monophonic melodies and are composed in *chanson-rustique* fashion, while the newer works generally employ polyphonic models and often have two equal upper voices.

## The *Tiers livre de chansons* Printed by Le Roy and Ballard (1553[22])

### *The Anthology*

The dissemination of the chanson during the second half of the sixteenth century owed much to the association of Adrian Le Roy and Robert Ballard in Paris. They issued their first edition in 1551, and by 1553 their firm had received the official designation "Imprimeurs du Roy," a title formerly held by the publishing house of Pierre Attaingnant. Although Le Roy and Ballard also issued volumes of religious and instrumental music, their chief output consisted of secular vocal works, of which almost two thousand were chansons.[19]

Books of three-part chansons were in the minority by 1550, but Le Roy and Ballard printed several volumes of pieces in this disappearing genre. Some of their three-voice anthologies contained compositions then current, other collections were retrospective, and a few volumes were devoted to works by a single composer. The *Tiers livre de chansons* is unusual, relative to the other chansonniers of Le Roy and Ballard. They published this print, measuring 170 × 230 mm., in choirbook format, and this was contrary to their usual practice of issuing such collections in partbooks. Although its title indicates that this volume was the third book of a series, there are no other extant volumes to supply further information about the nature of that series.[20] Indeed, the main sequence of numbered anthologies published by Le Roy and Ballard, a sequence that concentrated on four-part chansons, had its own "third" book.

The three-part compositions in the *Tiers livre de chansons* of 1553 are grouped by mode.[21] Such modal arrangements generally imply the presence of an editor well versed in music—in this case the lutanist Adrian Le Roy. In this print the highest part of several chansons appears on the upper right-hand page of an opening. This is unusual in choirbook format, because traditionally the highest part is notated on the upper left. To facilitate performance, these parts have been exchanged in the transcription when necessary, and a citation of this exchange has been made in the Critical Commentary.

### *The Music and Composers*

Like the Gardane prints, the Le Roy and Ballard anthology of twenty-six works contains a mixture of styles and composers (six pieces are, in fact, concordant with those in Gardane's editions—Part II, nos. 2, 9, 12, 13, 20, and 23 LRB). The presence of "Fors seullement la mort" and "Amy, souffrez que je vous aime"[22] (Part II, nos. 11 and 19 LRB), two of the most successful chansons from the early part of the century (both were composed before 1520), suggests that popularity may have been a factor determining the selection of chansons for the anthology. At this time three-part chansons were sometimes converted into the more current medium of four voices by adding a newly composed line to the unaltered original work. As many as three different such versions (known as *si placet* settings) exist for "Amy, souffrez"; its many concordances and numerous adaptations thus provide ample testimony to the work's appeal. Although "Amy, souffrez" is composed in an up-to-date style similar to that of "Amour, Amour, tu es par trop cruelle" (Part I, no. 8), Févin's "Fors seullement" is old-fashioned, with its long note values, numerous melismas, avoidance of full cadences, and general linear independence. Gascongne's "Beuvons, ma commere" (Part II, no. 10 LRB), composed in the *chanson-rustique* style of about 1515, is probably also one of the older chansons in the print.

Several of the works are written for two rival (i.e., equal) superius parts (Part II, nos. 4, 5, 6, 7, 17, 18, 22, and 23 LRB), a style that was in vogue about 1535, when Attaingnant's *Trente et une chansons* (see above) appeared with chansons composed for this fashionable combination of voices. In only one of these newer chansons in the Le Roy and Ballard anthology (Part II, no. 18 LRB) does the lowest of the three parts go below c, and in several cases the lowest note is even higher; it descends only to the f that is a fourth above c. As the century progressed, this preference for higher third parts became increasingly apparent in the three-part repertoire. The inclusion of three pieces for three superius parts (Part II, nos. 12, 13, and 21 LRB) in the *Tiers livre de chansons* is further evidence of the preference for higher voice parts. A number of these three-voice pieces were derived from four-voice models.

The opening work in Le Roy and Ballard's print, "Pourtant si je suis brunette," composed by Pierre de Villiers and set to a text by Marot (with some alterations), relates musically to the second chanson in the same collection, "Je suis trop jeunette" by Gascongne (see Part I, no. 26 for this chanson; it first appears in Gardane's 1541 collection and is, therefore, transcribed only in Part I). In setting "Pourtant si je suis brunette," De Villiers made an explicit musical connection with "Je suis trop jeunette" by duplicating the opening notes of all three voices of Gascongne's setting; however, this relationship does not continue beyond the incipit of "Pourtant si je suis brunette." Pierre de Villiers is associated with Lyons on the basis of his many pieces in prints of Moderne and his setting of a text in Lyonnaise dialect.

The works in this anthology by the three composers who resided in Italy (Gardane, Willaert, and Arcadelt) all show a marked individuality. Gardane's "N'avons point veu mal assenée" (Part II, no. 24 LRB) is based on the same popular text and melody used by Richafort in a chanson published in *La Couronne et fleur* (1536[1]). The strong preference that Gardane exercised for low ranges in his capacity as editor is reflected in his own work. Compared to the other pieces in the Le Roy and Ballard print, Gardane's low F in the bass is unusual.

Willaert's canon "Si je ne voy m'amie" (Part II, no. 26 LRB) is deliberately positioned as the last piece in the source-anthology. The appearance of a canon on the final *verso* occurs occasionally in other chansonniers as well, since fewer parts need to be notated, and they can thus be placed on a single page without crowding. This canon may have come from Willaert's younger years, perhaps from about 1520, when a number of his canons were published; the repetitions within the work and the undistinguished quality of the writing suggest it was composed early in his career. The popular character of the text and melody of two other works attributed to Willaert, "Allons, allons gay" and "La rousée du mois de may" (Part II, nos. 3 and 8 LRB), suggests a borrowed *cantus firmus*. "La rousée" (attributed to both Richafort and Willaert) shows elements of *chanson-rustique* style and was probably composed around 1515, while the more syllabic setting of "Allons, allons gay" indicates a later date of composition.[23]

The four chansons by Arcadelt (Part II, nos. 14, 15, 16, and 25 LRB) are probably among the newest in the Le Roy and Ballard collection.[24] Their style contrasts dramatically with the other works in the *Tiers livre* in the following ways: (1) the texture is consistently homophonic, with two superius parts that maintain the interval of a third through much of the writing; (2) the range of the two upper parts is often narrow, relative to that of the other chansons in the collection; (3) the lowest voice moves in a relatively high register; (4) triple meter, used only occasionally during the first half of the sixteenth century, characterizes three of the four chansons; (5) the texts are treated syllabically and include additional verses. Arcadelt was among the first composers to write in this homophonic style, which later achieved success as the *air de cour* during the second half of the century. The simple, direct quality of Arcadelt's chansons may have prompted the inclusion of "Je ne veux plus" (Part II, no. 14 LRB) with the incipit "Dieu est regnart" in a later book of devotional *contrafacta* (1577[2]).

Hilaire Penet's two chansons (Part II, nos. 5 and 17 LRB) contain both old and new features and in all likelihood were written shortly before 1535. Penet's death date is unknown, but Attaingnant published no new works by him after 1534. Both pieces have the rival superius parts typical of chanson composition about 1535. However, "Il fait bon" (Part II, no. 17 LRB) is based on a monophonic chanson, a practice that suggests an early composition date;[25] and "Au joly bois" (Part II, no. 5 LRB) borrows from a four-part chanson by Claudin, but it duplicates the melody most closely in the tenor, which is an old-fashioned location for the *cantus firmus*.

Hesdin's two contributions to the *Tiers livre* also show mixed characteristics. Both illustrate the crossing superius parts and a high third voice. "Mon pere m'a tant batu" (Part II, no. 4 LRB) is composed on a popular text and maintains a homorhythmic style, whereas "Il n'est soulas" (Part II, no. 22 LRB) is a more courtly imitative setting. Hesdin, alias Nicolle des Celliers, died in 1538.

The remaining chansons in Le Roy and Ballard's anthology were probably composed after 1538. Robert Meigret's chanson "Puis que de vous" (Part II, no. 18 LRB) is unusual in that it represents the only three-part chanson known to be written by this composer. The piece is an adaptation from a four-part model by Sandrin, with the superius duplicated quite closely. Since Marot's text for "Puis que de vous" was not published until 1538 in Lyons, the work probably did not originate much before that date, although musical settings occasionally preceded text publication, as noted above.

The text for De Bussy's chanson "Qui vauldra sçavoir" (Part II, no. 6 LRB) also appeared for the first time in 1538, in a chanson by Sandrin from which De Bussy borrowed the tenor. Works by De Bussy are contained in French publications issued between 1553 and 1583; otherwise, little is known of this composer. "Vray Dieu qu'amoureux ont de peine!" (Part II, no. 21 LRB) is attributed in this source to Belin and in a later print (1578[14]) to De Bussy. Not enough information is available about either musician to support a choice of one composer over the other. However, the only chansons known to be by Belin were for four voices and were composed in a chordal style, quite unlike the present work. Whether the piece was written by Belin or De Bussy, it is still counted among the later contributions to the *Tiers livre* for two reasons. First, it uses three high voices, a distribution popular around 1535; and, second, no works by either composer appeared in print before 1538. Du Buisson's "L'autre jour" (Part II, no. 7 LRB) seems to be based on the tenor melody of a four-voice chanson by Certon on the same text, but the latter piece was not published until 1550. Du Buisson's three-part setting employs crossing superius parts and a lowest voice that does not descend below f. The work falls, therefore, among the later works in Le Roy and Ballard's anthology.

Le Roy and Ballard's collection is significant not only for the four *unica* it contains (Part II, nos. 10, 18, 22, and 24 LRB), but also for its cosmopolitan character. The pieces in this anthology span a period from the first decade of the sixteenth century up to 1550. There is something for everyone: older chansons; *chansons rustiques*; chansons in the "Parisian" chordal style; newer chansons with rival superius parts; pieces with three high ranges; a canon; and, finally, the prophetic three-part works of Arcadelt. The print contains both popular and courtly poems in almost equal numbers, and it includes four texts by known poets, two by Marot (Part II, nos. 1 and 18 LRB) and two by Mellin de Saint-Gelais (Part II, nos. 16 and 25 LRB).

## Sources and Editorial Methods

The source for the chansons of Part I of this edition, Gardane's *Di Constantio Festa il primo libro . . .* (1541[13]), is complete only at the Accademia filarmonica in Verona. The tenor part from a slightly altered later version (1543[23]) is held by the Staatliche Bibliothek, Eichstätt, Germany.

The second source-anthology, Gardane's *Primo libro di madrigali d'Archadelt a tre voci . . .* (1543[21]), exists in complete form only in the Österreichische Nationalbibliothek in Vienna (a tenor part is also held by the Biblioteca municipal in Madrid). Gardane's curious custom of rearranging the contents and adding or subtracting a few pieces before bringing out subsequent editions has resulted in the fact that no other print issued by him is identical to this 1543 publication. However, three other editions are very similar to it. These are as follows: (1) An earlier version (1542[18]) with a slightly different title contains the same basic corpus of compositions, but it includes some madrigals by Festa and has three fewer motets and one less chanson. The chansons in this publication of 1542 are ordered differently and placed between the madrigals and motets instead of at the end of the book. This 1542 source is available complete at the Accademia filarmonica in Verona. (2) A later version (1559[21]) with a similar title adds an "Agnus Dei" by Layolle and makes some changes in the composer-attributions for the motets. (3) One final edition (1587[8]) contains the same compositions as our source anthology of 1543, but reverses the order of the third and fourth madrigals; this 1587 print was issued by the rival firm of Girolamo Scotto, also of Venice.

The third collection that is transcribed in the present edition is the *Tiers livre de chansons . . .*, issued by Le Roy and Ballard (1553[22]). This source is available in only one copy, which may be found complete at the Bibliothèque Mazarine in Paris.

Except for the chansons by Claudin and Arcadelt, available in the *Opera omnia* editions for these composers, only a few of these three-part chansons have appeared in modern editions, and they are located in various isolated sources.[26]

As noted above, seven chansons in this edition appear twice among the three source-prints. In order to retain the original character of the sources as much as possible, this edition lists the titles of duplicate chansons in the table of contents of each volume and refers the reader to the place the transcription may be found. These "duplicate chansons" all appear in the sources for Part II of this edition (see no. 9 Gardane; 2, 9, 12, 13, 20, and 23 LRB). Although those chansons in the later anthologies that also appear in an earlier one will not be repeated in the musical section of this edition, they are given separate numbers.

The only major musical changes that have been made in this edition involve the transposition of several chansons. Sixteen of the thirty chansons in Gardane's book of 1541 and one in his book of 1543 appear at pitches below those found in concordances. These works have been transcribed at the higher pitches found in the other sources; however, Gardane's incipit at the beginning of these special pieces has been retained in this edition to show his lower pitch level. The two upper parts of eight pieces in the *Tiers livre* printed by Le Roy and Ballard have been exchanged to better reflect their relationship, and mention has been made of this in the Critical Commentary.

Note values have been reduced by half in the transcriptions, and fermatas have been added to the final notes where they are lacking in the source (i.e., throughout $1541^{13}$ and $1543^{21}$ and in some of the parts of $1553^{22}$). There is no differentiation between written-out repeats occurring at the end of a chanson and repeats indicated by a *signum congruentiae*; both are expressed by means of modern repeat signs here.

Other editorial emendations to the underlaid text and music include the following: (1) Inconsistencies of spelling among the three parts have been standardized but not corrected. (2) Adjustments from "i" to "j" and between "v" and "u" have been made, and acute accents have been added. Any *grave* accents that appear in the edition are also present in the source. Cedillas have been added where necessary. (3) Capital letters have been added when needed at the beginning of poetic lines, in the case of proper names and "Dieu," and in some instances of direct address, such as "Amour." (4) Minimal punctuation has been incorporated. (5) Repetitions of text indicated in the source by "ij" have been placed in angled brackets; editorial additions appear in square brackets. (6) The spelling of composers' names has been standardized according to general usage. (7) The ampersand and other abbreviations have been expanded tacitly, and elisions of text have been indicated. (8) Mensural emendations by the editor appear in brackets. Occasionally when a repeat is involved at the end of a piece, modern notation requires a meter change to avoid repeating a half measure. The indication of (3/2) in these places is for notational convenience in modern transcription and does not mean the composer intended a change to triple meter (Part I, nos. 5 and 15; Part II, nos. 3 and 4 Gardane, and nos. 4, 6, 18, and 19 LRB). (9) Coloration ( ⌐ ¬ ) and ligatures ( ⌐—¬ ) have been incorporated in the music. (10) Editorial accidentals have been indicated above the staff on the basis of a judicious weighing of the following principles. Those principles enumerated first take precedence when a conflict occurs. At cadences and significant junctures within the piece, perfect intervals are approached by the closest imperfect consonance in stepwise progressions. The tritone has been avoided both melodically and harmonically insofar as possible at primary points in the work, but it still occurs sometimes in connection with passing tones. Accidentals that appear in concordances have generally been included. The B (and occasionally the E) has been flatted when it represents the peak of a melodic line. False relations have been avoided; and when possible in a succession of imitative entries, an effort has been made to maintain the same intervalic relationship of half-tones and whole-tones among the entries. The editorial accidentals apply only to the note directly beneath them.

## Acknowledgments

I would like to express my appreciation to a number of people who made valuable contributions to the preparation of this edition. I am especially grateful to Prof. Mary S. Lewis of the Massachusetts Institute of Technology, who sent me sections of her dissertation on Gardane prior to its availability on microfilm. Dr. Sarah Spence of Columbia University kindly provided many perceptive comments on the translations and did much to improve them. To Prof. Norman Smith of the University of Pennsylvania go my special thanks for his suggestions regarding mensuration issues of the sixteenth century. I owe a long-standing debt of gratitude to Profs. Lawrence F. Bernstein and Alvin H. Johnson, both of the University of Pennsylvania. Their generosity in sharing with me their specialized knowledge of this repertoire has proved invaluable. My appreciation is also due Prof. Daniel Heartz of the University of California at Berkeley for correspondence relating to the *Trente et une chansons* of Attaingnant, an important source of concordances for this edition. Finally, I'd like to thank Dottóre Enrico Paganuzzi of the Accademia filarmonica in Verona for his kindness and help.

Courtney S. Adams
January 1982 Franklin and Marshall College

# Notes

1. Lawrence F. Bernstein, "The 'Parisian Chanson': Problems of Style and Terminology," *Journal of the American Musicological Society* XXXI (1978): 193-240.

2. For example, Arcadelt's "Je ne sçay que c'est qu'il me fault" and his "Quand viendra la clarté" (Part II, nos. 16 and 25 LRB) are set to texts by Saint-Gelais. Hubert Daschner, who identifies a number of poets in these source-anthologies, suggests that Saint-Gelais may also be the author of a text used by Cosson ("Voyant souffrir celle qui me tormente," Part II, no. 5 Gardane); see Daschner, *Die gedruckten mehrstimmigen Chansons von 1500-1600: Literarische Quellen und Bibliographie* (Bonn, 1962), p. 172.

3. Lawrence F. Bernstein, "Claude Gervaise as Chanson Composer," *Journal of the American Musicological Society* XVIII (1965): 381.

4. For biographical information about Gardane, see Mary S. Lewis, "Antonio Gardane and His Publications of Sacred Music, 1538-55" (Ph.D. diss., Brandeis University, 1979). Concerning the Gardane firm, see Claudio Sartori, "Una dinastia di editori musicali," *La Bibliofilia* LVIII (1956): 176-208.

5. These include a print of four-part chansons, mainly devoted to Janequin (1538[19]); a book of duos, most of which were composed by Gardane (1539[21]); some duos primarily by Gero (1541[14]); an anthology of duos (1543[19]); and two volumes containing three-part chansons (1541[13] and 1542[18]).

6. François Lesure, "Les Chansons à trois voix de Clément Janequin," *Revue de musicologie* XLIV (1959): 193-198.

Thomas Bridges, author of the "Gardane" article in Stanley Sadie, ed., *The New Grove Dictionary of Music and Musicians* (1980), has suggested to this editor another interpretation of the error. He believes that the title page of the 1541 edition was too transparently incorrect, at least in regard to Festa, to be a deliberate attempt to deceive. Since Gardane's Italian customers would have recognized the fraud immediately, Bridges suspects that the mix-up may have come about through a confusion of title pages in the printing shop. He also notes that since Gardane's source for the Janequin chansons is uncertain, it could have been Gardane who was himself deceived.

7. Catherine Chapman, "Andrea Antico" (Ph.D. diss., Harvard University, 1964), p. 164.

8. Lewis, "Antonio Gardane," p. 229.

9. To Claudin de Sermisy, Attaingnant ascribed chansons numbered in Part I of this edition as 3-6, 11, 13, 18, 22, 23, 27, and 30; Le Heurteur is credited with nos. 2 and 17 (Part I), Gosse with nos. 15 and 29 (Part I), and Gascongne with no. 26 (Part I). The two concordances without attribution in Attaingnant's print are nos. 8 and 12 (Part I).

10. For a discussion of this Attaingnant print of 1535 and the reliability of the attributions to Claudin, see Daniel Heartz, "*Au pres de vous*—Claudin's Chanson and the Commerce of Publishers' Arrangements," *Journal of the American Musicological Society* XXIV (1971): 193-225; and Courtney S. Adams, "Some Aspects of the Chanson for Three Voices during the Sixteenth Century," *Acta musicologica* IL (1977): 236-237. For information on Claudin, see Isabelle Cazeaux, "The Secular Music of Claudin de Sermisy" (Ph.D. diss., Columbia University, 1961).

11. Biographical information for this composer and others discussed in the Preface comes from Stanley Sadie, ed., *The New Grove Dictionary of Music and Musicians; Die Musik in Geschichte und Gegenwart* (Kassel: Bärenreiter, 1957); and Bernstein, "The 'Parisian Chanson,' " unless otherwise stated.

12. Barton Hudson does not even include this piece among the dubious works of Ninot le Petit, since the style is at such variance with Ninot's other chansons. See Barton Hudson, ed., *Ninot le Petit: Collected Works*, Corpus mensurabilis musicae, 87.

13. William McMurtry, "The British Museum Manuscript Additional 35087: A Transcription of the French, Italian and Latin Compositions with Concordance and Commentary" (Ph.D. diss., North Texas State University, 1967), p. 12.

14. Samuel F. Pogue, *Jacques Moderne: Lyons Music Printer of the Sixteenth Century* (Geneva, 1969), p. 46.

15. The monophonic version appears as no. 29 in Théodore Gérold, ed., *Le Manuscrit de Bayeux* (Paris, 1921), p. 32.

16. Howard Mayer Brown describes the *chanson rustique* style in "The Genesis of a Style: The Parisian Chanson, 1500-1530" in *Chanson and Madrigal 1480-1530*, ed. James Haar (Cambridge, Mass., 1964), pp. 20-24.

17. These versions include an anonymous setting in Brussels MS 228 (modern edition in Martin Picker, *The Chanson Albums of Marguerite of Austria* [Berkeley and Los Angeles, 1965], pp. 410-412), an anonymous arrangement in Attaingnant's *Quarante et deux chansons* (1529[4]; modern edition by Bernard Thomas, ed., *The Parisian Chanson*, Vol. X [London, 1977]: 21), and a version by Gascongne in Cambridge MS 1760 (modern edition in Howard Mayer Brown, *Theatrical Chansons of the Fifteenth and Early Sixteenth Centuries* [Cambridge, Mass., 1963], pp. 92-94).

18. Although there is no model extant for "Dame d'honneur, princesse de beaulté," in all likelihood one once existed.

19. François Lesure and Geneviève Thibault, *Bibliographie des éditions d'Adrian Le Roy et Robert Ballard (1551-1598)* (Paris, 1955), p. 20.

20. François Lesure speculates that there is a missing volume of duos and trios by Janequin that was probably published by Le Roy and Ballard in 1551. Conceivably, this collection of pieces may belong with the *Tiers livre*. A. Tillman Merritt and François Lesure, eds., *Clément Janequin (c. 1485-1558)*; Chansons polyphoniques, vol. 1 (Paris, 1956), p. vi.

21. The first eleven chansons are in the Dorian mode; these are followed by two in the Aeolian mode and another in Dorian. The next eleven pieces are in the Ionian mode, and the last one in Mixolydian. Transposed and untransposed modes are intermingled.

22. Of the four composers who may have written this chanson (Claudin de Sermisy, Isaac, Le Heurteur, and Moulu), Lawrence Bernstein supports the attribution to Isaac. Bernstein, "Notes on the Origin of the 'Parisian' Chanson" (Paper presented at the forty-sixth annual meeting of the American Musicological Society, Denver, Colorado, 7 November 1980). Bernstein rules out Claudin and Le Heurteur for bibliographic reasons. (Their names do not ap-

pear on the music, only in the tables of contents.) Although the style of "Amy, souffrez que je vous aime" is not typical of either Moulu or Isaac, there is a composition by Isaac that shows similar characteristics in the opening and closing sections (see Johannes Wolf, ed., *Heinrich Isaac: Weltliche Werke*, I, Denkmäler der Tonkunst in Österreich, XXVII, no. 53 [Graz, 1959], p. 121).

23. For a discussion of Willaert's chanson style and its chronology, see Lawrence F. Bernstein, "*La Courone et fleur des chansons a troys*: A Mirror of the French Chanson in Italy in the Years between Ottaviano Petrucci and Antonio Gardano," *Journal of the American Musicological Society* XXVI (1973): 1-68. The conflicting attributions of "La rousée" to Richafort and Willaert are evaluated in Lawrence F. Bernstein, ed., *La Couronne et fleur* (New York: Broude Bros. Ltd., forthcoming).

24. The large number of chansons by Arcadelt that appeared in prints published in 1553 and afterwards suggests that his return to France from Italy (occurring sometime between 1552 and 1557) probably took place about 1553 or shortly before.

25. The three-part setting alters the textual incipit, but the tune is the same. See "On doibt bien aymer" in Gérold, *Le Manuscrit de Bayeux*, p. 13, and in Gaston Paris and Auguste Gevaert, eds., *Chansons du XV$^{e}$ Siècle* (Paris, 1875), no. 109.

26. A recent publication by Albert Seay, *Jacques Moderne: Le Parangon des chansons, Quart livre [1538]* (Colorado Springs, 1981), provides concordances for ten chansons in a modern edition: Nos. 6, 9, 12, 13, 14, 15, 22 (with a mistaken attribution to Mouton), and 30 from Gardane's 1541 print, "Il est en vous" from Gardane's 1543 volume and LeRoy and Ballard's book, and "Allons, allons gay" from the latter print. The chansons of Claudin have been edited as vols. III-IV of Claudin's *Opera Omnia*, Corpus mensurabilis musicae, 52; those of Arcadelt appear in Arcadelt's *Opera Omnia*, Corpus mensurabilis musicae, 31, vol. III, edited by Albert Seay. Joseph Schmidt-Görg has included "Je suis trop jeunette" (Part I, no. 26) in his edition of Nicolas Gombert's *Opera Omnia*, Corpus mensurabilis musicae, 6, vol. IX.

"C'est malencontre que d'aymer" (Part I, no. 24) and "Allons, allons gay" (Part II, no. 3 LRB) may be found in Howard Mayer Brown, *Theatrical Chansons of the Fifteenth and Early Sixteenth Centuries* (Cambridge, Mass., 1963), pp. 25-27 and 3-5, respectively; "Quant je boy du vin" (Part I, no. 17) appears in Maurice Cauchie, *Trente Chansons à trois et quatre voix de Clément Janequin* (Paris, 1928), pp. 43-46; "Amy, souffrez que je vous aime" (Part II, no. 19 LRB) is transcribed in several sources, including, among others, Albert Seay, ed., *Pierre Attaingnant: Transcriptions of Chansons for Keyboard*, Corpus mensurabilis musicae, 20; and the Claudin *Opera Omnia* cited above.

# Critical Commentary for Part I

Minimal variations among concordances that involve cadential ornamentation, the addition or subtraction of a tie in transcription, or the replacement of a larger note value with two or more smaller ones at the same pitch (and *vice versa*) have not generally been recorded. Occasionally, if several sources deviate consistently, even these small changes are documented in the commentary. The editor has omitted from the Critical Commentary obvious errors in the concordances, variations in text underlay and spelling, and indications of ligatures or coloration. Mentioned in the Commentary are alterations of accidentals and any note changes other than those found in standard cadential formulas. *Si placet* settings are listed after the concordances; but the *si placet* settings have not been compared note-by-note with the chanson in the source-anthology. Conflicting attributions have been listed with the concordant sources in which they appear. The list of references following a composer's name or the word "anonymous" identifies the source in which the attribution is made. Such attributions are particularly relevant to the first thirty chansons below, which Gardane misattributed to Janequin in two prints ($1541^{13}$ and $1543^{23}$).

The full titles and locations of the concordant manuscripts and prints consulted for this edition are given below under Sources for Concordant Readings. In listing the concordances that apply for each work, RISM numbers are used where possible; "Heartz-65" refers to book No. 65 in the catalogue of Attaingnant's prints published by Daniel Heartz, and "LT-67" indicates print No. 67 in the catalogue of Le Roy and Ballard's editions issued by François Lesure and Geneviève Thibault. Concordances are referred to in the Critical Commentary by means of the designations given them under Sources for Concordant Readings. Inclusive pages and folios are cited for the primary source-anthologies; references to concordances and *si placet* settings list the first page or folio of the upper part only.

The following abbreviations are used: S. = upper part; T. = middle voice; B. = lowest part; m. (mm.) = measure (measures); c′ = middle C. Changes in notes are described by measure, voice-part, and note, followed by the name of the appropriate concordance. Notes (whether tied or not) are counted from the beginning of each measure, so that "M. 3, B., notes 4-6 are all eighth-notes (a′, b′, c″)" means that in m. 3 of the bass part, notes 4 through 6 appear in the concordance as a′, b′, c″ in eighth-notes on the treble staff. For convenience, modern equivalents are used in referring to note values.

*Sources for Concordant Readings*

MANUSCRIPTS

| | |
|---|---|
| Basel 59-62 | Basel, Universitätsbibliothek, MSS F. IX. 59-62. (Part II, no. 19 LRB, *si placet* setting *à* 4.) |
| Cambrai 125-128 | Cambrai, Bibliothèque municipale, MSS 125-128. (Part I, no. 28, *si placet* setting *à* 4.) |
| Cambridge 1760 | Cambridge, Magdalene College, MS Pepys 1760. (Part I, no. 16; Part II, no. 11 LRB.) |
| Copenhagen 1848 | Copenhagen, Kongelige Bibliotek Ny Kgl. Samling MS 1848-2°. (Part II, no. 11 LRB.) |
| Florence 117 | Florence, Biblioteca Nazionale Centrale, MS Magl. XIX. 117. (Part I, no. 16; Part II, no. 19 LRB.) |
| Heilbronn X.2 | Heilbronn, Heilbronner Gymnasial-Bibliothek, MS X.2. (Bass only.) (Part I, no. 28.) |
| London 5242 | London, British Museum, MS Harley 5242. (Part I, no. 16.) |
| London 29380 | London, British Museum, Add. MS 29380. (Part II, no. 3 LRB.) |
| London 29381 | London, British Museum, Add. MS 29381. (Part I, nos. 8 and 28.) |
| London 31922 | London, British Museum, Add. MS 31922. (Transcribed by John Stevens, *Music at the Court of Henry VIII*, Vol. XVIII of *Musica* |

| | |
|---|---|
| | *Britannica* [London, 1962].) (Part II, nos. 11 and 19 LRB.) |
| London 35087 | London, British Museum, Add. MS 35087. (Part I, no. 28.) |
| Munich 1516 | Munich, Bayerische Staatsbibliothek, Mus. MS 1516. (Part I, no. 28; Part II, nos. 8 and 11 LRB; no. 19 LRB, *si placet* setting *à 4*.) |
| Regensburg 940/41 | Regensburg, Proske-Bibliothek, MS A.R. 940/41. (Part II, no. 19 LRB, *si placet* setting *à 4*.) |
| Saint Gall 463 | St. Gall, Stiftsbibliothek, Cod. 463. (Tschudi Liederbuch, Superius only.) (Part II, no. 11 LRB.) |
| Turin I. 27 | Turin, Biblioteca Nazionale, Riserva Musicale, MS I.27. (Part I, no. 24.) |
| Ulm 236 | Ulm, Bibliothek des Münsters, Schermar'sche Sammlung, MSS $236^{a\text{-}d}$. (Part II, no. 19 LRB, *si placet* setting *à 4*.) |
| Ulm 237 | Ulm, Bibliothek des Münsters, Schermar'sche Sammlung, MSS $237^{a\text{-}d}$. (Part I, no. 28.) |
| Uppsala $76^a$ | Uppsala, Universitetsbiblioteket, MS $76^a$. (Part I, no. 16.) |

PRINTS

| | |
|---|---|
| Heartz-65 | *Trente et une chansons musicales*. Paris, Attaingnant, 1535. (Primus Superius only.) (Part I, nos. 2-6, 8, 11-13, 15, 17, 18, 22, 23, 26, 27, 29, and 30; Part II, nos. 2, 3, 7, 9, 11, and 13 Gardane; nos. 2, 12, 13, 20, and 23 LRB.) |
| LT-67 | *Cincquiesme livre de chansons*. Paris, Le Roy and Ballard, 1560. (Part II, nos. 3, 8, and 26 LRB.) |
| $1520^6$ | *Chansons a troys*. Venice, Antico and Giunta. (Superius and Bass only.) (Part I, nos. 7 and 24; Part II, no. 11 LRB.) |
| $1529^4$ | *Quarante et deux chansons*. Paris, Attaingnant. (Part II, no. 19 LRB.) |
| $1536^1$ | *La Couronne et fleur des chansons a troys*. Venice, Antico and del-l'Abbate. (Part II, nos. 3 and 8 LRB.) |
| $1538^9$ | *Trium vocum carmina*. Nuremberg, Formschneider. (Part I, nos. 7 and 28; Part II, no. 11 LRB.) |
| $1539^{19}$ | *Le Parangon des chansons*. Lyons, Moderne. (Part I, nos. 6, 9, 12-15, 22, and 30; Part II, no. 7 Gardane; nos. 3, 9, and 12 LRB.) |
| $1540^7$ | *Selectissimae necnon familiarissimae cantiones*. Augsburg, Kriesstein. (Part I, no. 4; Part II, no. 8 LRB.) |
| $1541^2$ | *Trium vocum cantiones centum*. Nuremberg, Petreius. (Part I, nos. 4, 8, 11, 16, 18, and 23; Part II, nos. 8, 11, 13, and 23 LRB.) |
| $1541^{13}$ | *Di Constantio Festa il primo libro*. Venice, Gardane. (Part II, no. 9 Gardane; nos. 2, 9, 13, 20, and 23 LRB.) |
| $1542^8$ | *Tricinia*. Wittenberg, Rhau. (Part I, no. 7; Part II, no. 19 LRB.) |
| $1542^{18}$ | *Primo libro di madrigali d'Archadelt a tre voci*. Venice, Gardane. (Part I, no. 29; Part II, nos. 1-11 and 13 Gardane; no. 12 LRB.) |
| $1543^{21}$ | *Primo libro di madrigali d'Archadelt a tre voci*. Venice, Gardane. (Part I, no. 29; Part II, no. 12 LRB.) |
| $1543^{23}$ | *Quaranta madrigali di Jhan Gero*. Venice, Gardane. (Tenor only.) (Part I, nos. 1-30; Part II, no. 9 Gardane; nos. 2, 9, 13, 20, and 23 LRB.) |
| $1552^{10}$ | *La Fleur de chansons et cinquiesme livre*. Antwerp, Susato. (Part I, no. 26; Part II, no. 2 LRB.) |
| $1552^{11}$ | *La Fleur de chansons et sixiesme livre*. Antwerp, Susato. (Bass only.) (Part II, no. 2 Gardane.) |
| $1553^{22}$ | *Tiers livre de chansons*. Paris, Le Roy and Ballard. (Part I, nos. 2, 11, 14, 18, and 26; Part II, no. 7 Gardane.) |
| $1559^{21}$ | *Il primo libro di madrigali d'Archadelt*. Venice, Gardane. (Part I, no. 29; Part II, nos. 1-13 Gardane; no. 12 LRB.) |

[1560]$^{1}$ *Selectissimorum triciniorum*. Nuremberg, Berg and Neuber. (Part I, nos. 4 and 18; Part II, nos. 19 and 23 LRB.)

1560$^{2}$ *Variarum linguarum tricinia*. Nuremberg, Berg and Neuber. (Part I, no. 26; Part II, no. 2 LRB.)

1560$^{7}$ *Premier livre du recueil des fleurs*. Louvain, Phalèse. (Part II, no. 10 Gardane.)

1562$^{9}$ *Il terzo libro delle muse a tre voci*. Venice, Scotto. (Superius only.) (Part II, no. 2 Gardane; nos. 3 and 8 LRB.)

1569$^{9}$ *Recueil des fleurs produictes de la divine musicque*. Louvain, Phalèse. (Part II, no. 10 Gardane.)

1569$^{11}$ *Recueil des fleurs produictes de la divine musicque*. Louvain, Phalèse. (Part I, no. 26; Part II, nos. 2 and 3 LRB.)

1573$^{15}$ *Chansons a troys parties de M. Jaques Arcadet*. Paris, Le Roy and Ballard. (Part II, nos. 14-16 and 25 LRB.)

1574$^{3}$ *La Fleur des chansons a trois parties*. Louvain, Phalèse and Bellère. (Part II, no. 8 Gardane; no. 3 LRB.)

1577$^{2}$ *Premier livre du meslange des pseaumes*. [Geneva, Saint-André]. (Part II, no. 14 LRB, with incipit "Dieu est regnart.")

1578$^{14}$ *Premier livre de chansons a trois parties*. Paris, Le Roy and Ballard. (Part I, no. 11; Part II, nos. 2 and 7 Gardane; nos. 4, 5, 11-13, 17, 19, and 21 LRB.)

1578$^{15}$ *Second livre de chansons a trois parties*. Paris, Le Roy and Ballard. (Part I, nos. 14, 26, and 30; Part II, nos. 1, 2, and 6-9 LRB.)

1578$^{16}$ *Tiers livre de chansons a trois parties*. Paris, Le Roy and Ballard. (Part I, no. 25; Part II, nos. 3 and 8 LRB.)

1587$^{8}$ *Di Archadelt il primo libro*. Venice, Scotto. (Bass only.) (Part I, no. 29; Part II, nos. 1-13 Gardane; no. 12 LRB).

*Three-Part Chansons Printed by Gardane (1541$^{13}$)*

All the works in this source and its concordance, 1543$^{23}$, contain erroneous attributions to Janequin. The composers listed after the title are those cited in other concordances; if no other concordances exist or if they are without ascription, then the composer attribution appears as "anonymous."

[1] JENNETTE, MARION SE VONT JOUER (Anonymous)

Primary Source—1541$^{13}$, p. 37.

Concordant Source—1543$^{23}$ (tenor only), p. 35.

No variants.

[2] REGRETZ, SOUCY ET PEINE (Le Heurteur—Heartz-65, 1553$^{22}$)

Primary Source—1541$^{13}$, p. 38.

Concordant Sources—Heartz-65, fol. ix$^{r}$; 1543$^{23}$ (tenor only), p. 54; 1553$^{22}$, fols. 22$^{v}$-23$^{r}$.

Pitch—As transcribed: Heartz-65; 1553$^{22}$. At the lower fifth: 1541$^{13}$; 1543$^{23}$.

M. 13, B., note 4-m. 14, beat 1, B., these notes rendered as a single half-note in 1541$^{13}$; changed here by analogy with 1553$^{22}$, for better text underlay. M. 17, B., note 1 is flatted in 1553$^{22}$. M. 30, B., note 1 is flatted in 1553$^{22}$.

[3] C'EST UNE DURE DESPARTIE (Claudin—Heartz-65)

Primary Source—1541$^{13}$, pp. 38-39.

Concordant Sources—Heartz-65, fol. ix$^{v}$; 1543$^{23}$ (tenor only), p. 42.

Pitch—As transcribed: Heartz-65. At the lower fifth: 1541$^{13}$; 1543$^{23}$.

No variants.

[4] JE NE FAIS RIEN QUE REQUÉRIR (Claudin—Heartz-65)

Primary Source—1541$^{13}$, p. 39.

Concordant Sources—Heartz-65, fol. vii$^{v}$; 1540$^{7}$, no. 89; 1541$^{2}$, no. 56; 1543$^{23}$ (tenor only), p. 42; [1560]$^{1}$, no. 26.

Pitch—As transcribed: Heartz-65. At the lower fifth: all other concordances, which probably came from a print by Gardane, judging from the erroneous attribution to Janequin.

Composer attribution is to Janequin in 1540$^{7}$, 1541$^{2}$, 1543$^{23}$, and [1560]$^{1}$. In Gardane's reprint (1543$^{23}$), the tenor partbook contains the superius part, a better reflection of their relationship. M. 10, S., notes 3 and 4 rendered as a single quarter-note (c') in 1540$^{7}$, 1541$^{2}$, and [1560]$^{1}$.

[5] CELLE QUI M'A TANT POURMENÉ (Claudin—Heartz-65)

Primary Source—1541$^{13}$, p. 40.

Concordant Sources—Heartz-65, fol. v$^{v}$; $1543^{23}$ (tenor only), p. 41.

Pitch—As transcribed: Heartz-65. At the lower fifth: $1541^{13}$; $1543^{23}$.

No significant variants.

[6] Au pres de vous secretement demeure (Claudin—Heartz-65, $1539^{19}$)

Primary Source—$1541^{13}$, p. 41.

Concordant Sources—Heartz-65, fol. vi$^{v}$; $1539^{19}$, fol. 29; $1543^{23}$ (tenor only), p. 54.

Pitch—As transcribed: Heartz-65; $1539^{19}$. At the lower fifth: $1541^{13}$; $1543^{23}$.

No variants.

[7] Tant est gentil, plaisant et gracieulx (Anonymous)

Primary Source—$1541^{13}$, p. 42.

Concordant Sources—$1520^{6}$, fol. 9$^{r}$; $1538^{9}$, no. 51; $1542^{8}$, no. 67; $1543^{23}$ (tenor only), p. 44.

M. 10, B., notes 2-4 are quarter- and two eighth-notes in $1538^{9}$. M. 15, S., notes 3-5 are quarter- and two eighth-notes in $1538^{9}$. M. 19, T., note 2 has flat in $1542^{8}$. M. 21, B., note 1 has flat in $1538^{9}$. M. 22, S., notes 1-3 are quarter- and two eighth-notes in $1538^{9}$. M. 29, T., notes 2-4 are quarter- and two eighth-notes in $1538^{9}$. M. 29, S., note 2-m. 30, note 3, these notes rendered as half- and two eighth-notes (a′ g′ f′) in $1538^{9}$. M. 32, T., note 5-m. 33, note 4, these notes rendered as two half-notes (a c′) in $1542^{8}$. M. 42, S., note 7-m. 43, note 2 rendered as quarter-note (b′) and two eighths (a′ g′) in $1538^{9}$.

[8] Amour, Amour, tu es par trop cruelle (Anonymous—Heartz-65)

Primary Source—$1541^{13}$, pp. 42-43.

Concordant Sources—London 29381, fol. 41$^{r}$; Heartz-65, fol. ii$^{v}$; $1541^{2}$, no. 88; $1543^{23}$ (tenor only), p. 44.

The erroneous attributions to Janequin in London 29381 and $1541^{2}$ probably come from a print by Gardane.

No other variants.

[9] Mauldicte soit la mondaine richesse (Cosson—$1539^{19}$)

Primary Source—$1541^{13}$, p. 43.

Concordant Sources—$1539^{19}$, fol. 32; $1543^{23}$ (tenor only), p. 43.

No variants.

[10] La loy d'amours est tant inique et dure (Anonymous)

Primary Source—$1541^{13}$, p. 44.

Concordant Source—$1543^{23}$ (tenor only), p. 46.

No significant variants.

[11] Contre raison vous m'estes fort estrange (Claudin—Heartz-65, $1553^{22}$, $1578^{14}$)

Primary Source—$1541^{13}$, pp. 44-45.

Concordant Sources—Heartz-65, fol. xiii$^{v}$; $1541^{2}$, no. 92; $1543^{23}$ (tenor only), p. 46; $1553^{22}$, fols. 14$^{v}$-15$^{r}$; $1578^{14}$, fol. 17$^{r}$.

Pitch—As transcribed: Heartz-65; $1553^{22}$; $1578^{14}$. At the lower fifth: $1541^{2}$; $1541^{13}$; $1543^{22}$.

Composer attribution to Janequin in all parts of $1541^{2}$ except the bass part, which attributes this piece to Gero. In both of their prints ($1553^{22}$ and $1578^{14}$) Le Roy and Ballard have exchanged the two upper parts. M. 10, T., notes 2-3 rendered as four eighth-notes (g′ f′ g′ a′) in $1553^{22}$ and $1578^{14}$. M. 17, B., notes 2-4 rendered as a single half-note (f′) in $1578^{14}$. Mm. 30 and 35, S., notes 3-6 rendered as dotted-quarter and eighth-note (d″ e″) in $1578^{14}$. M. 35, S., notes 1-2 are both e″; changed here by analogy with $1553^{22}$ and $1578^{14}$ to avoid parallel fifths with B.

[12] Le cueur de vous ma présence désire (Anonymous—Heartz-65, $1539^{19}$)

Primary Source—$1541^{13}$, p. 45.

Concordant Sources—Heartz-65, fol. ii$^{r}$; $1539^{19}$, fol. 28; $1543^{23}$ (tenor only), p. 45.

M. 2, B., note 3 has no flat in $1539^{19}$. M. 16, B., note 1 has no flat in $1539^{19}$.

[13] J'ay le désir content et le faict resolu (Claudin—Heartz-65, $1539^{19}$)

Primary Source—$1541^{13}$, p. 46.

Concordant Sources—Heartz-65, fol. v$^{r}$; $1539^{19}$, fol. 22; $1543^{23}$ (tenor only), p. 43.

Pitch—As transcribed: Heartz-65; $1539^{19}$. At the lower fifth: $1541^{13}$; $1543^{23}$.

In $1539^{19}$ Moderne has exchanged the two upper parts. M. 24, T., notes 3-6 rendered as a dotted-quarter and eighth-note (e′ f′) in $1543^{23}$. M. 31, S., note 2 rendered as two eighth-notes (g′ f′) in $1539^{19}$. M. 32, T., notes 1-2 rendered as a single half-note (d″) in $1543^{23}$. The text for this chanson has also been attributed to François I, Marguerite of Navarre (his sister), and Mellin de Saint-Gelais on the basis of additional manuscript sources.

[14] Grace et vertu, bonté, beaulté, noblesse (Le Heurteur—$1553^{22}$, $1578^{15}$; Anonymous—$1539^{19}$)

Primary Source—$1541^{13}$, p. 47.

Concordant Sources—$1539^{19}$, fol. 27; $1543^{23}$ (tenor only), p. 37; $1553^{22}$, fols. 10$^{v}$-11$^{r}$; $1578^{15}$, fol. 14$^{v}$.

No significant variants.

[15] Amour, me voyant sans tristesse (Gosse—Heartz-65, $1539^{19}$)

Primary Source—$1541^{13}$, p. 48.

Concordant Sources—Heartz-65, fol. iiii$^{r}$; $1539^{19}$, fol. 24; $1543^{23}$ (tenor only), p. 40.

Pitch—As transcribed: Heartz-65; $1539^{19}$. At the lower fifth: $1541^{13}$; $1543^{23}$.

M. 25, S. and T., there are parallel fifths between these parts in this m. M. 36, T., note 1 omitted in $1541^{13}$ and $1543^{23}$; added here by analogy with $1539^{19}$.

[16] HELLAS, JE SUIS MARRY DE CES MAULDITZ JALEUX (Févin—Cambridge 1760, Uppsala $76^{a}$, modern hand; Anonymous—Florence 117, London 5242)

Primary Source—$1541^{13}$, p. 49.

Concordant Sources—Cambridge 1760, fol. li$^{v}$; Florence 117, fol. l$^{v}$; London 5242, fol. 24$^{v}$; Uppsala $76^{a}$, fol. 47$^{v}$; $1541^{2}$, no. 86; $1543^{23}$ (tenor only), p. 36.

Composer attribution is to Janequin in $1541^{2}$. M. 1, all parts, extra half-measure of rest inserted at beginning of piece in Cambridge 1760, Florence 117, London 5242, and Uppsala $76^{a}$. M. 2, T., notes 1-2 rendered as a quarter-note (a) in Cambridge 1760; B., note 3 rendered as a quarter and two eighth-notes (g f e) in Florence 117 and Uppsala $76^{a}$. M. 7, S., notes 2-4 rendered as quarter and two eighth-notes in Florence 117 and Uppsala $76^{a}$; T., notes 2-4 rendered as quarter and two eighth-notes in Florence 117 and Uppsala $76^{a}$. M. 7, B., note 6-m. 8, note 2, these notes rendered as four eighth-notes (f e f g) in Florence 117 and Uppsala $76^{a}$. M. 8, S., notes 2 and 3 are dotted quarter and eighth in Cambridge 1760, Florence 117, and Uppsala $76^{a}$. M. 9, S., note 1 rendered as two eighth-notes (f′ e′) in Florence 117. M. 13, T., notes 1-3 are a quarter- and two eighth-notes in Florence 117, London 5242, and Uppsala $76^{a}$. M. 14, S., notes 1-3 rendered as quarter and two eighth-notes in Florence 117 and Uppsala $76^{a}$; T., note 2-m. 15, note 1 rendered as dotted half (c′), quarter (c′) in Florence 117 and Uppsala $76^{a}$. M. 16, S., note 3 is a in Cambridge 1760, Florence 117, London 5242, and Uppsala $76^{a}$. M. 17, B., notes 1-4 rendered as two half-notes (g d) in Cambridge 1760. M. 17, S., note 5-m. 18, note 5, these notes rendered as a half-note (d′) followed by a quarter-note (c′) in Cambridge 1760, Florence 117, London 5242, and Uppsala $76^{a}$. M. 18, S., note 6-m. 19, note 1, these notes rendered as a half-note (d′) followed by a whole-rest in Cambridge 1760, Florence 117, and Uppsala $76^{a}$. M. 19, T., beats 1-3 rendered as half-note (a), quarter-rest, quarter-note (d′) in Cambridge 1760. M. 22, B., note 2 is f in Cambridge 1760. M. 23, S., note 2 rendered as dotted quarter and eighth-note (b a) in London 5242. M. 28, S., note 1 rendered as two eighth-notes (b a) in Florence 117 and Uppsala $76^{a}$. M. 29, B., notes 2 and 3 rendered as dotted quarter (g), two eighths (f f), and two sixteenths (e d) in Cambridge 1760. M. 33, S., note 5-m. 34, note 5, these notes rendered as half-note (g) followed by quarter-note (f) in Cambridge 1760, Florence 117, London 5242, and Uppsala $76^{a}$. M. 36, T., note 5 rendered as two eighths (a g) in $1543^{23}$. M. 37, S., note 1 rendered as two eighth-notes (b a) in Florence 117 and Uppsala $76^{a}$. M. 38, B., notes 2 and 3 rendered as dotted quarter (g), quarter (f), eighth (f), and two sixteenths (e d) in Cambridge 1760. M. 42, S., note 5-m. 43, note 5, these notes rendered as half-note (g) followed by quarter-note (f) in Cambridge 1760, Florence 117, London 5242, and Uppsala $76^{a}$; T., notes 2 and 3 rendered as dotted quarter (c′) and three eighths (b a g) in Florence 117 and Uppsala $76^{a}$. M. 43, B., note 2-m. 44, note 5, these notes rendered as eight eighth-notes (G A G A B c d c) in Florence 117 and Uppsala $76^{a}$. M. 44, S., notes 1 and 2 are both quarter-notes in London 5242, and notes 1-5 are rendered as eight eighth-notes (d′ c′ d′ e′ f′ e′ d′ e′) in Florence 117 and Uppsala $76^{a}$. M. 45, S., note 3 rendered as three eighth-notes (a′ b′ a′) in Florence 117 and Uppsala $76^{a}$.

[17] QUANT JE BOY DU VIN CLARET TOUT TOURNE (Le Heurteur—Heartz-65)

Primary Source—$1541^{13}$, p. 50.

Concordant Sources—Heartz-65, fol. x$^{v}$; $1543^{23}$ (tenor only), p. 55.

No significant variants.

[18] VIGNON, VIGNON, VIGNON, VIGNETTE (Claudin—Heartz-65, $1553^{22}$)

Primary Source—$1541^{13}$, p. 51.

Concordant Sources—Heartz-65, fol. xiii$^{r}$; $1541^{2}$, no. 70; $1543^{23}$ (tenor only), p. 50; $1553^{22}$, fols. 25$^{v}$-16$^{r}$ [26$^{r}$]; $[1560]^{1}$, no. 40.

Pitch—As transcribed: Heartz-65; $1553^{22}$. At the lower fourth: $1541^{2}$; $1541^{13}$; $1543^{23}$; $[1560]^{1}$.

Composer attribution to Janequin (probably from a Gardane source) in $1541^{2}$ and $[1560]^{1}$. There is no repeat of the final phrase in $1553^{22}$. M. 9, B., note 3 is c′ in $1553^{22}$. M. 21, S., half-rest rendered as half-note (g′) in $1541^{2}$ and $[1560]^{1}$. M. 32, T., notes 3-4 rendered as a single quarter-note (e′′) that is supplied with a cautionary accidental indicating that the note should not be flatted in $1553^{22}$. M. 34, B., note 3 is c′ in $1553^{22}$.

[19] BASTIENNE, BASTIENNE, VOUS AVES CHANGÉ D'AMIS (Anonymous)

Primary Source—$1541^{13}$, p. 52.
Concordant Source—$1543^{23}$ (tenor only), p. 48.
No variants.

[20] Bon pastoreau, garde bien ta houlette (Anonymous)
Primary Source—$1541^{13}$, p. 53.
Concordant Source—$1543^{23}$ (tenor only), p. 49.
No significant variants, but note parallel fifths between the S. and T. at m. 6.

[21] La tres doulce plaisant velue (Anonymous)
Primary Source—$1541^{13}$, p. 54.
Concordant Source—$1543^{23}$ (tenor only), p. 47.
No variants. M. 26, T., notes 1-3 emended by the editor from half-note, quarter-note, quarter-note to avoid consecutive fourths.

[22] Par fin despit je m'en iray seullette (Claudin—Heartz-65, $1539^{19}$)
Primary Source—$1541^{13}$, pp. 54-55.
Concordant Sources—Heartz-65, fol. $xi^{r}$; $1539^{19}$, fol. 33; $1543^{23}$ (tenor only), p. 48.
Pitch—As transcribed: Heartz-65; $1539^{19}$. At the lower fourth: $1541^{13}$; $1543^{23}$.
M. 1, B., quarter-rest and note 1 rendered as a single half-note (a) in $1539^{19}$.

[23] Si mon malheur my continue (Claudin—Heartz-65)
Primary Source—$1541^{13}$, p. 55.
Concordant Sources—Heartz-65, fol. $v^{v}$; $1541^{2}$, no. 71; $1543^{23}$ (tenor only), p. 47.
Pitch—As transcribed: Heartz-65. At the lower fourth: $1541^{2}$; $1541^{13}$; $1543^{23}$.
Composer attribution to Janequin in $1541^{2}$. The two upper parts have been exchanged in Heartz-65. M. 16, S. and T., all sources have parallel octaves in this m. except $1541^{2}$, which has the pitch of note 5 of the S. as f''.

[24] C'est malencontre que d'aymer (Anonymous)
Primary Source—$1541^{13}$, p. 56.
Concordant Sources—Turin I. 27, fol. $44^{v}$ [new]; $1520^{6}$, fol. $9^{v}$; $1543^{23}$ (tenor only), p. 38.
Cadential variants are extensive in both Turin I. 27 and in $1520^{6}$. M. 15, B., note 3 is a dotted quarter and the eighth-rest is omitted in Turin I. 27. M. 22, T., note 1 is c' in all sources except Turin I. 27; the Turin reading is used here because it preserves the melodic contour. M. 29, T., note 2-m. 31, note 3, these notes rendered as three half-notes (f' e' d'), dotted quarter (c'), eighth (b), dotted quarter (e'), two eighths (d' d'), and two sixteenths (c' d') in Turin I. 27. M. 43, T., notes 1 and 2 are dotted half-note and quarter-note in Turin I. 27. M. 46, T., note 2 rendered as two eighth-notes (g f) in Turin I. 27. M. 56, B., note 3 rendered as a dotted quarter and eighth-note (d c) in Turin I. 27 and $1520^{6}$. M. 63, T., note 1 is f in $1541^{13}$; Gardane corrected this error in $1543^{22}$.

[25] En disant une chansonette (Gascongne—$1578^{16}$)
Primary Source—$1541^{13}$, p. 57.
Concordant Sources—$1543^{23}$ (tenor only), p. 51; $1578^{16}$, fol. $22^{v}$.
Pitch—As transcribed: $1578^{16}$. At the lower fourth: $1541^{13}$; $1543^{23}$.
M. 2, B., note 3 is c' in $1578^{16}$. M. 24, B., notes 1 and 2 rendered as a single quarter-note (a) in $1578^{16}$. M. 31, T., note 1 is a' in $1578^{16}$. M. 40, note 4-m. 41, note 3, S., these notes rendered as a single half-note (f') in $1578^{16}$ to avoid parallel octaves. M. 41, B., notes 2-3 rendered as a single quarter-note (f) in $1578^{16}$. M. 43, S., note 4 is b' and note 5 is a' in $1578^{16}$. M. 44, B., note 2 is f in $1578^{16}$.

[26] Je suis trop jeunette (Gascongne—Heartz-65, $1553^{22}$, $1578^{15}$; Gombert—$1552^{10}$ [bass only], $1560^{2}$, $1569^{11}$)
Primary Source—$1541^{13}$, p. 58.
Concordant Sources—Heartz-65, fol. $xi^{v}$; $1543^{23}$ (tenor only), p. 39; $1552^{10}$, fol. $21^{r}$; $1553^{22}$, fols. $2^{v}$-$3^{r}$; $1560^{2}$, no. 32; $1569^{11}$, p. 26; $1578^{15}$, fol. $6^{v}$.
Pitch—As transcribed: Heartz-65; $1553^{22}$; $1578^{15}$. At the lower fourth: $1541^{13}$; $1543^{23}$; $1552^{10}$; $1560^{2}$; $1569^{11}$.
The editor favors the attribution to Gascongne rather than Gombert. The earliest publication of the work in 1535 ascribes it to Gascongne. The attributions to Gombert were probably derived from Susato's print of $1552^{10}$, in which the name appears only in the bass partbook rather than in all three books, as was Susato's usual practice. The use of a monophonic chanson as *cantus firmus* in this work is also typical of Gascongne. M. 11, T., note 4 is f' in $1552^{10}$, $1560^{2}$, and $1569^{11}$. M. 41, T., note 4 is f' in $1552^{10}$, $1560^{2}$, and $1569^{11}$.

[27] J'ay contenté ma volunté suffisement (Claudin—Heartz-65)
Primary Source—$1541^{13}$, p. 59.
Concordant Sources—Heartz-65, fol. $viii^{v}$; $1543^{23}$ (tenor only), p. 52.
Pitch—As transcribed: Heartz-65. At the lower fourth: $1541^{13}$; $1543^{23}$.
The two upper parts are exchanged in Heartz-65.

Mm. 4-5, parallel fifths occur between the S. and B. in these mm. M. 27, S., note 1 and m. 31, S., note 1, flat in source has been editorially removed to avoid tritone.

[28] C'EST DONC POUR MOY QUE ANSINS SUIS FORTUNÉE (le Petit—London 29381; Willaert—Heilbronn X.2; Anonymous—London 35087, Munich 1516, Ulm 237, $1539^{8}$)

Primary Source—$1541^{13}$, p. 60.

Concordant Sources—Heilbronn X.2, no. 1; London 29381, fol. $35^{v}$; London 35087, fol. $81^{v}$; Munich 1516, no. 133; Ulm 237, fol. $23^{v}$; $1539^{8}$, no. 61; $1543^{23}$ (tenor only), p. 52.

*Si placet* setting—Cambrai 125-128, fol. $19^{r}$.

In the Formschneider print ($1539^{8}$) repeated notes are treated as single notes of longer value in numerous instances; this is appropriate to the instrumental implications of the lack of text in this source. M. 8, T., note 4 is b in $1539^{8}$; B., notes 3-4 rendered as two quarter-notes (d e) in Heilbronn X.2. M. 17, T., note 1 is rendered as a half-note and quarter-rest in London 35087, Munich 1516, Ulm 237, and $1539^{8}$; B., note 2 is g in Munich 1516. M. 17, S., note 2-m. 18, note 1, these notes rendered as half-note (b′) and quarter-rest in London 35087, Munich 1516, Ulm 237, and $1539^{8}$. M. 19, B., note 1 rendered as two quarter-notes (f d) in London 35087 and $1539^{8}$. M. 21, B., notes 1-5 rendered as two quarter-notes (d c) and a half-note (d) in Heilbronn X.2. M. 28, S., note 1 rendered as half-note (b′) and quarter-rest in Munich 1516. M. 47, T., notes 3-4 rendered as a single quarter-note (b) in London 35087, Munich 1516, Ulm 237, $1539^{8}$, and $1543^{23}$. M. 49, S., notes 1 and 2 are dotted quarter and eighth in Ulm 237; B., notes 3-4 are rendered as four eighth-notes (c d e f) in Heilbronn X.2 and Munich 1516. M. 49, B., note 4-m. 50, note 2, these notes rendered as a half-note (g) followed by a quarter-note (f) in $1539^{8}$.

[29] SI J'AY EU DU MAL OU DU BIEN (Gosse—Heartz-65; Ysoré—$1542^{18}$, $1543^{21}$, $1559^{21}$, $1587^{8}$)

Primary Source—$1541^{13}$, p. 61.

Concordant Sources—Heartz-65, fol. $iii^{r}$; $1542^{18}$, p. 20; $1543^{21}$, p. 27; $1543^{23}$ (tenor only), p. 53; $1559^{21}$, p. 27; $1587^{8}$, p. 21.

Pitch—As transcribed: Heartz-65; $1542^{18}$; $1543^{21}$; $1559^{21}$; $1587^{8}$. At the lower fourth: $1541^{13}$; $1543^{23}$.

No significant variants.

[30] CHANGEONS PROPOS, C'EST TROP CHANTÉ D'AMOURS (Claudin—Heartz-65, $1539^{19}$, $1578^{15}$)

Primary Source—$1541^{13}$, p. 62.

Concordant Sources—Heartz-65, fol. $vii^{v}$; $1539^{19}$, fol. 29 [26]; $1543^{23}$ (tenor only), p. 50; $1578^{15}$, fol. $12^{v}$.

Pitch—As transcribed: Heartz-65; $1539^{19}$; $1578^{15}$. At the lower fourth: $1541^{13}$; $1543^{23}$.

M. 26, S., notes 2-3 rendered as a single quarter-note (d′′) in $1578^{15}$. M. 32, S., notes 2-3 rendered as a single quarter-note (b′) in $1578^{15}$. M. 38, S., notes 3-6 rendered as a dotted quarter (a′) followed by an eighth-note (b′) in $1578^{15}$. M. 41, T., notes 3-4 rendered as a dotted quarter (a′) followed by an eighth-note (g′) in $1578^{15}$.

# Texts and Translations for Part I

## Three-Part Chansons Printed by Gardane ($1541^{13}$)

### [1]

Jennette, Marion se vont jouer aux champs,
Elle ont pleumé leur con poil a poil, en chantant,
Elle alloyent cerchant
Entre deux gabions
Pour i metre ung merchant
Qui feust bon compagnon
Et bon belaribon, bon, bon.

(Jennette and Marion went off to the fields to play,
They plucked themselves hair by hair, all the while singing,
They were going searching
Between two protective pillars
To put there a merchant
Who makes a good companion
And a good *belaribon, bon, bon*.)

### [2]

Regretz, soucy et peine
M'ont fait de villains tours,
Si pityé n'est soudaine,
Tost finiray mes jours;
Hellas, ce sont amours
Qui me font tout cecy,
J'ay bruit et renomée
D'avoir nouvel amy.

(Sorrow, care and pain
Have given me a base turn,
If pity does not come soon,
I will swiftly end my days;
Alas, it is love
That makes me thus,
I have passed the word about
That I have a new love.)

### [3]

C'est une dure despartie
De celuy ou j'ay mis mon cueur,
Dont m'en iray user ma vie
A l'hermitage de langueur;
Et tous les jours au matinet
Je m'en iray chanter sur la verdure,
Soubz le couvert d'ung buissonet,
La peine que pour luy je endure.

(It is cruel parting
From the one to whom I have given my heart,
From whom I will go away to spend
My life in isolated pining;
And every day in the morning
I will go singing on the green,
Under cover of a little bush,
Of the suffering that I endure for him.)

### [4] Clément Marot

Je ne fais rien que requérir
Sans acquérir
Le don d'amoureuse lyesse.
Las, ma maistresse,
Dictes quant esse
Qu'il vous plaira me secourir.
Je ne fais rien que requérir
Sans acquérir.

(I do nothing but search
Without finding
For the reward of love's joy.
Alas, my love,
Tell me when
It will please you to help me.
I do nothing but search
Without finding.)

**[5]** Clément Marot

Celle qui m'a tant pourmené
A eu pitié de ma langueur;
Dedans son jardin m'a mené
Ou tous arbres sont en vigueur;
Adoncques me usa sa rigueur.
Si je la baise, elle m'acolle,
Puis m'a donné son noble cueur,
Dont il m'est advis que je volle.

(She who led me on so
Took pity on my misery;
She led me into her garden
Where all the trees are in full strength;
Then she practiced on me her force.
Thus, I kiss her, she embraces me,
Then she gave me her noble heart,
From which I think I may take flight.)

**[6]**

Au pres de vous secretement demeure
Mon povre cueur sans que nul le conforte,
Et si languis pour la douleur qui porte,
Puis que voulés qu'en ce tourment il meure.

(Near to you secretly lives
My poor heart with nothing to comfort it,
And so I languish from the sorrow it bears,
Since you wish that in this torment it die.)

**[7]**

Tant est gentil, plaisant et gracieulx,
Plain de tous biens plus que rien soubz les cieulx;
Le cueur remply d'amour vray et perfaict
Que par honneur ne désyre en son faict
Fors bien aymer et hayr vicieulx.

(So much is noble, pleasing and favorable,
Full of all riches more than anything under the skies;
A heart filled with true and perfect love
That requires no chivalric deed
Except to love well and hate with malice.)

**[8]**

Amour, Amour, tu es par trop cruelle.
Quant tes amantz qui ne pensent que a bien,
Tu n'en sçays rien; mais mon cueur le sçaict bien,
Se amour me prent, c'est chose naturelle.

(Love, Love, you are too cruel.
As for your lovers who think only of the good,
You know nothing of it; but my heart knows well
If love possesses me, it is natural.)

**[9]** Clément Marot

Mauldicte soit la mondaine richesse
Qui m'a osté ma dame et ma maistresse,
Las, par vertu j'ay son amitié aquise,
Mais par richesse ung aultre l'a conquise;
Vertu n'a pas en amour grant prouesse.

(Accursed be worldly riches
Which have wooed from me my lady and my mistress,
Alas, through virtue I won her friendship,
But by wealth another has conquered her;
Virtue has little power in matters of love.)

**[10]**

La loy d'amours est tant inique et dure,
La passion si doulce sans mesure
Qu'elle me sforse suyvre jusque a la mort,
Que chascun jour me faict injure et tort
Et suis content du malheur que j'endure.

(The law of love is so unjust and cruel,
The passion so sweet without measure
That it compels me to follow unto death,
So that each day brings me injury and hurt
And I am content with the misfortune I endure.)

**[11]**

Contre raison vous m'estes fort estrange.
Ese bien faict; en aures vous louenge,
D'ainsy m'avoir soudain déshérité
De vostre amour sans l'avoir mérité?
Vous faict il mal sea vous servir me renge?

(Unfairly you are very harsh towards me.
Is it well done; will you be praised for it,
For thus having suddenly disinherited me
From your love without [my] having deserved it?
Does it harm you if I give myself to your service?)

**[12]** Clément Marot

Le cueur de vous ma présence désire,
Mais pour le mieulx belle je me retire,
Car sans avoir aultre contentement

Je ne pourroys servir si longuement.
Venons au point qu'on ne ose dire.

(Your heart my presence desires,
But it is better, my beauty, that I withdraw,
For without having other pleasure
I would not be able to serve so long.
Let us come to what one dares not say.)

### [13] Claude Chappuys ?

J'ay le désir content et le faict resolu.
J'ay le sçavoir certain car Amour l'a voulu
Par quoy je tiens mon bien de l'heureuse pensée
En tres bien le gardant que ne soit offensée,
Dont pour ma liberté a altrui m'abandonne
Que le moins de son plus trop myeulx que moy me donne.

(I have the happy desire and the deed resolved.
I have sure knowledge for Love has wished it
By which I retain a happy spirit,
In guarding it very well that it not be harmed,
Whereby for my liberty I yield myself to others
For the least they can do is care more than I do.)

### [14]

Grace et vertu, bonté, beaulté, noblesse
Sont a m'amye point ne le fault celer;
Trop me desplaict d'en ouyr mal parler,
Je hay celluy qui l'honneur d'elle blesse.

(Grace, virtue, goodness, beauty, and nobility
Belong to my love, make no secret of it;
I am much displeased to hear ill spoken of her,
I hate anyone who wounds her honor.)

### [15] Clément Marot

Amour, me voyant sans tristesse
Et de le servir desgouté,
M'a dict que je feisse une maistresse
Et qu'il seroit de mon costé.
Apres l'avoir bien escouté,
J'en ay faict une a ma plaisance;
Et ne me suis point mesconté,
C'est bien la plus belle de France.

(Love, seeing me without sorrow
And displeased with serving him,
Has told me to take a mistress
And that he would be on my side.
After having listened well,
I have taken one who pleases me;
And I have not erred,
She is indeed the most beautiful in France.)

### [16]

Hellas, je suis marry de ces mauldítz jaleux
Qui ont sur moy si grant fantesie,
Leur femmes n'ont bonne heure ne demye,
Hellas, il leur sembloit que je en fusse amoureulx.

(Alas, I am weary of those cursed jealous fools
Who weave such fantasy about me,
Their women have no happiness at all,
Alas, it seemed to them that I was in love with them.)

### [17]

Quant je boy du vin claret tout tourne,
Et quant je n'en boy point tout ne tourne point,
Et quant n'ay maille ne denier je ne boyt point,
Ne belle fille a mon coucher tout ne tourne point.
Et quant de ces vins blancs je boy
Si ne sont d'Anjou ou d'Arboys, point ne me tourne;
Quant je boy du vin claret tout tourne.

(When I drink claret everything goes round,
And when I don't drink it, nothing goes round,
And when I have neither halfpenny nor copper I don't drink,
Nor have a pretty girl in my bed, nothing goes round.
And when white wines I drink
If not from Anjou or Arbois, nothing makes me go round;
When I drink claret everything goes round.)

### [18]

Vignon, vignon, vignon, vignette,
Qui te planta il fust preudhom.
Tu fuz coupée a la serpette,
Vignon, vignon, vignon, vignette,
Il me semble advis que j'alecte
Quant tu passes mon gorgeron.
Vignon, vignon, vignon, vignette,
Qui te planta il fust preudhom.

(Vine, vine, vine, little vine,
The one who planted you was a wise man.
You were cut with the vine hook,
Vine, vine, vine, little vine,
I think that I may like it

As you pass down my throat.
Vine, vine, vine, little vine,
The one who planted you was a wise man.)

**[19]**

Bastienne, Bastienne, vous avés changé d'amis
Vous aves laissé Guillaume pour prendre petit Denis,
Il ne vous fringuera pas, sur mon ame, Bastienne.
Bastienne, Bastienne, quant le rose florirunt
Garde bien sur vous mammelles s'il y a point de boutons,
Et garde bien vostre con qu'on ni entre, Bastienne.

(Bastienne, Bastienne, you have changed lovers
You have left Guillaume to take little Denis,
He will not have you, upon my soul, Bastienne.
Bastienne, Bastienne, when the roses bloom
Keep them well over your breasts so there are no nipples,
And guard yourself well that no one enters, Bastienne.)

**[20]**

Bon pastoreau, garde bien ta houlette
Pour défendre des mauldítz loups rabis
Tes doulx agneaulx, moutons beaulx et brebis
Qui sont tous nuds tondus retem a pillette.

(Good father, keep close your shepherd's crook
To protect from the evil rabid wolves
Your gentle lambs, beautiful sheep and ewes
Who are all bare, shorn, and kept plucked.)

**[21]**

La tres doulce plaisant velue
Sallit l'autrier en mi la rue
Parée d'ung vert cotton,
Ainsy disoyt en son jargon:
Qui en veult je ne mord ne rue.

(The sweet pleasing girl with all the hair
Accosted me the other day in the street
Dressed in green cotton,
Thus she said in her dialect:
"Who wants some, I neither bite nor put to flight.")

**[22]**

Par fin despit je m'en iray seullette
Au joly boys a l'ombre d'ung buisson,
En attendant passer ma marrisson
Et que j'auray ma volunté parfaicte.

(From vexation I will go off alone
To the pretty woods under the shade of a little bush,
While waiting for my grief to pass
And to have perfect contentment.)

**[23]**

Si mon malheur my continue,
Je ne sçay pas,
Je ne dis pas que je feray;
A tout le moins je changeray
Si le couraige ne my mue.

(If my unhappiness continues,
I know not,
I cannot say what I will do;
At the very least I will change
If my heart does not forsake me.)

**[24]**

C'est malencontre que d'aymer
Qui n'en a joye,
Qui veult d'amour sçavoir le cours:
Amours font faire maints détours
Et engendrer couroux et plours
Donc je larmoye
Par ung quidam qui nuit et jour
Si mi guerroye.
C'est malencontre que d'aymer
Qui n'en a joye.

(It is a misfortune that the one who loves
Has no joy from it,
Who wishes to know the way of love:
Love requires many detours
And causes grief and lamentation
From which I weep because of someone
Who night and day
Fights me so.
It is a misfortune that the one who loves
Has no joy from it.)

**[25]**

En disant une chansonette
Je vire une dame brunette,
Allaquelle pour alberger
Je dis, me volés vous loger
En nuit en vostre maisonette?

(While singing a little song
I dance about a dark-haired lady,
To whom for shelter
I say, "Do you wish to put me up
For the night in your little house?")

**[26]**

Je suis trop jeunette
Pour faire ung amy.
Si suis je bien preste
D'en faire ung joly,
S'il est a ma poste,
Il aura mon cueur.
Je layray mon pere,
Ma mere, mon frere, ma seur,
M'en iray seulette
Au boys avec lui
Cuillir violette
Pour passer ennuy.

(I am too young
To take a lover.
But I am ready
To take a gallant,
If he is to my liking,
He will have my heart.
I will leave my father,
My mother, my brother, my sister,
I will go off alone
To the woods with him
To gather violets
To pass the time away.)

**[27]** Clément Marot

J'ay contenté ma volunté suffisement
Car j'ay esté d'amours traicté diversement.
J'ay eu tourment, bon traictement,
J'ay eu doulceur et cruaulté,
Et ne me plains fors seullement
D'avoir aymé si loyaulment
Celle qui est sans loyaulté.

(I have satisfied my desire sufficiently
For I have been treated by love diversely.
I have had torment, good treatment,
I have had sweetness and cruelty,
And do not complain except for
Having loved so faithfully
One who is without loyalty.)

**[28]**

C'est donc pour moy que ansins suis fortunée;
Infortune, hellas, suis sur ma foy
Plus malheureuse au monde n'est que moy;
Aultre que moy n'est de telle heure née.

(So it is that I am thus fated;
Unfortunate, alas, I am indeed
The most unhappy creature in the world;
No other was born to such a fortune.)

**[29]**

Si j'ay eu du mal ou du bien
Par oubli ou par souvenir,
Je ne me veulx plaindre de rien.
Dieu me doit mieulx a l'advenir,
Mais je vous prie de retenir
Desormais en vostre pensée
Qu'amityé qui se peult finir
Ne fut jamais bien commencée.

(If I have received evil or goodness
Through forgetfulness or remembering,
I do not wish to complain of anything.
God owes me better in the future,
But I beg you to keep
Henceforth in your thoughts
That a friendship which can be ended
Was never well begun.)

**[30]** Clément Marot

Changeons propos, c'est trop chanté d'amours;
Ce sont clamours, chantons de la serpette.
Tours vignerons ont a elle recours,
C'est le secours pour tailler la vignette.
O serpillette, O la serpillonnette,
La vignollette est par toy mise sus
Dont les bons vins tous les ans sont yssus.

(Let us change our song, too much is sung of love;
That is noise, let us sing of the pruning knife.
All vineyard keepers have recourse to it,
It is of help to cut the little vine.
O little knife, O very little knife,
The little vine is by you made to fall
Whereby good wines every year are produced.)

CANTUS
DI CONSTANTIO FESTA
IL PRIMO LIBRO DE MADRIGALI A TRE VOCI,
Con la Gionta de Quaranta Madrigali di IHAN GERO, Nouamente ristampato, & da molti errori emendato, Aggiuntoui similmente Trenta Canzoni Francese di Ianequin.
.A. .G.
CONCORDES VIRTVTE ET NATVRA MIRACVLIS
M. D. XLI.
Excudebat Venetiis, Apud Antonium Gardane.

Plate I. *Di Constantio Festa il primo libro de madrigali a tre voci, . . . Aggiuntovi similmente Trenta Canzoni Francese di Janequin*. Venetiis: Antonium Gardane, 1541.
Cantus partbook. Title page. (Courtesy of the Accademia filarmonica, Verona)

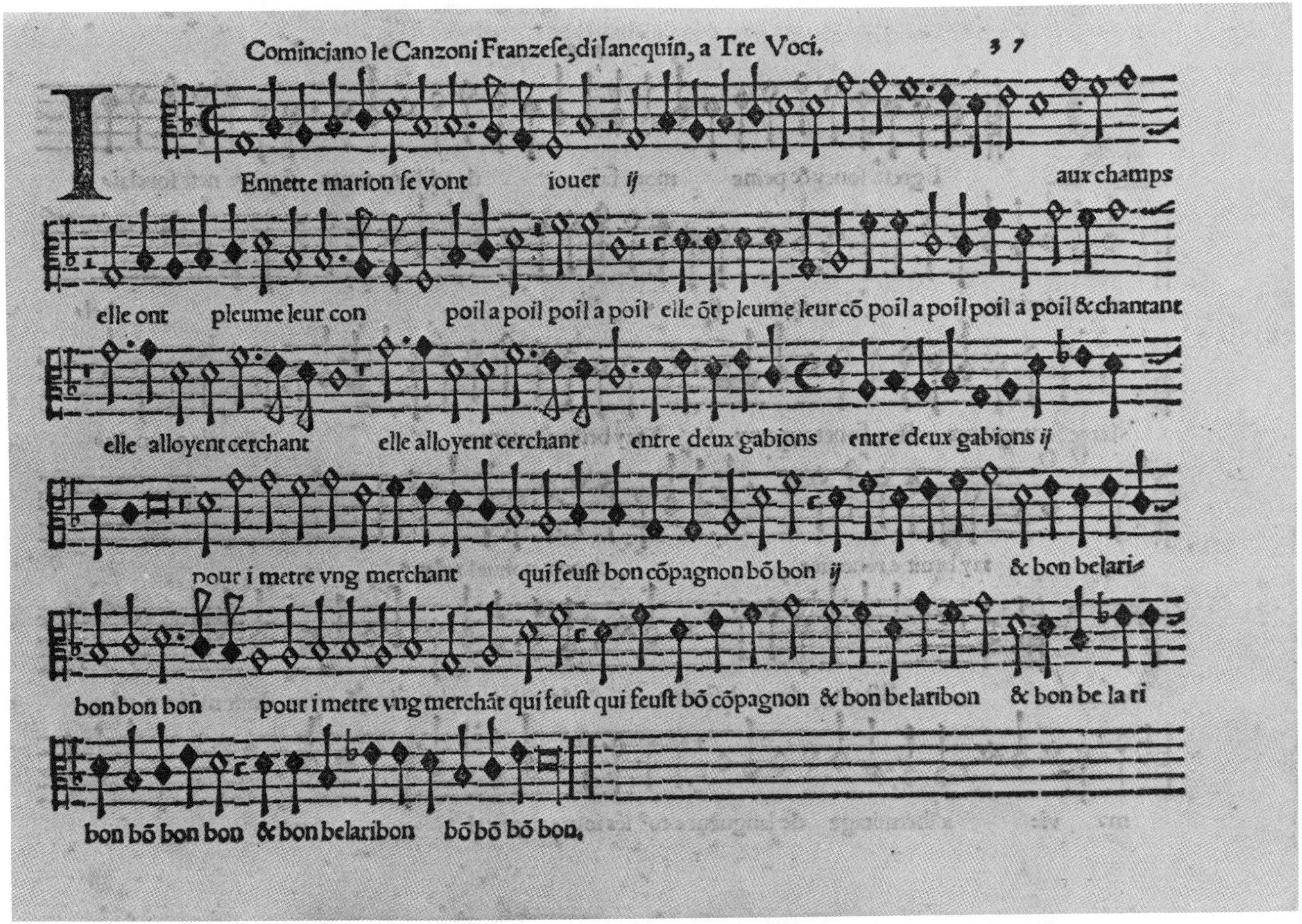
Cominciano le Canzoni Franzese, di Ianequin, a Tre Voci.
37
I
Ennette marion se vont iouer ij aux champs
elle ont pleume leur con poil a poil poil a poil elle ōt pleume leur cō poil a poil poil a poil & chantant
elle alloyent cerchant elle alloyent cerchant entre deux gabions entre deux gabions ij
pour i metre vng merchant qui feust bon cōpagnon bō bon ij & bon belari
bon bon bon pour i metre vng merchāt qui feust qui feust bō cōpagnon & bon belaribon & bon be la ri
bon bō bon bon & bon belaribon bō bō bō bon.

Plate II. *Di Constantio Festa il primo libro de madrigali a tre voci, . . . Aggiuntovi similmente Trenta Canzoni Francese di Janequin*. Venetiis: Antonium Gardane, 1541.
Cantus partbook. Page 37. (Courtesy of the Accademia filarmonica, Verona)

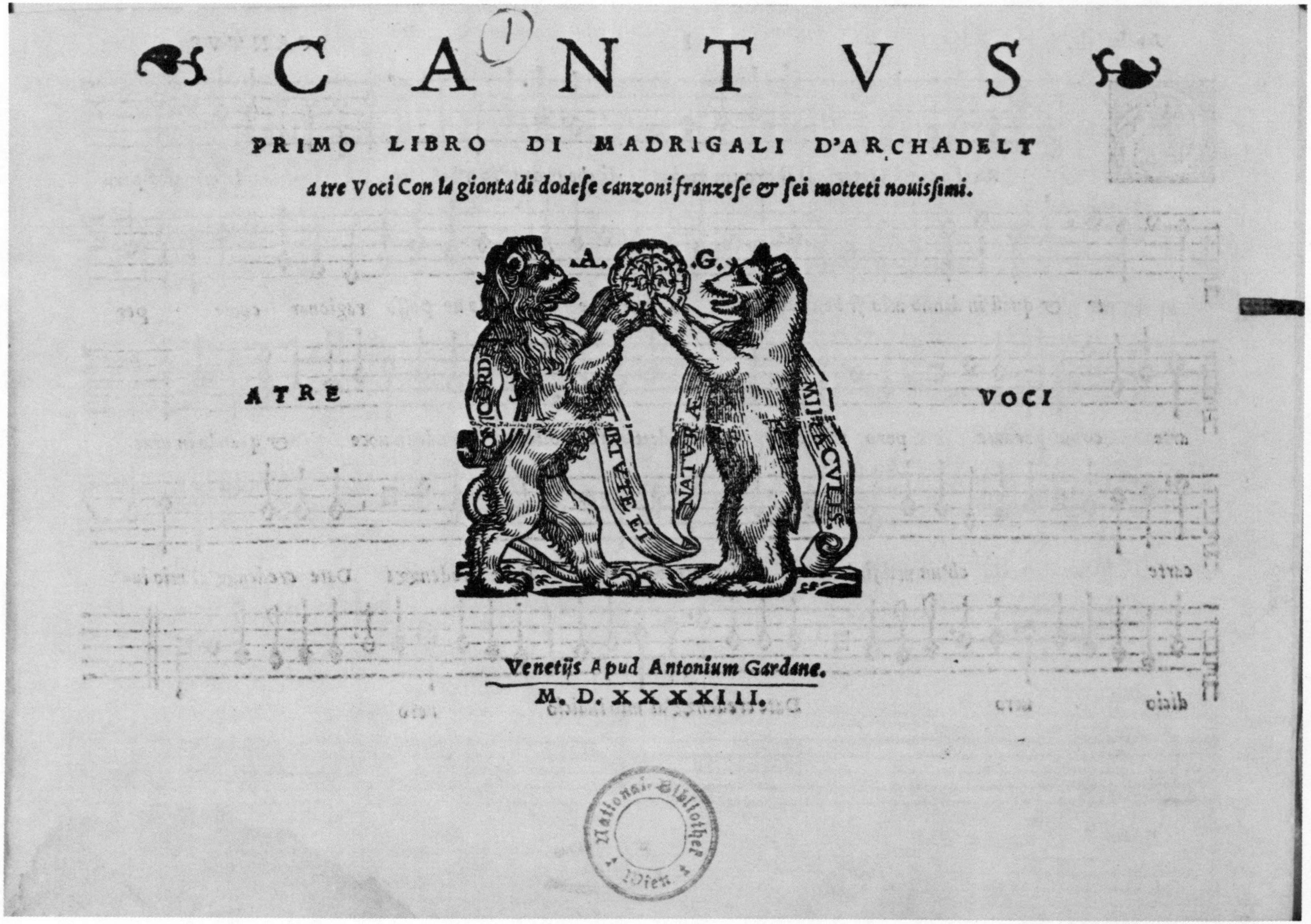

CANTVS

PRIMO LIBRO DI MADRIGALI D'ARCHADELT

a tre Voci Con la gionta di dodese canzoni franzese & sei motteti nouissimi.

.A. .G.

ATRE VOCI

CONCORDI

VIRTVTE ET

NATVRÆ

MIRACVLIS

Venetijs Apud Antonium Gardane.

M. D. XXXXIII.



Plate III. *Primo libro di madrigali d'Archadelt*. Venetiis: Antonium Gardane, 1543. Cantus partbook. Title page. (Courtesy of the Österreichische Nationalbibliothek).

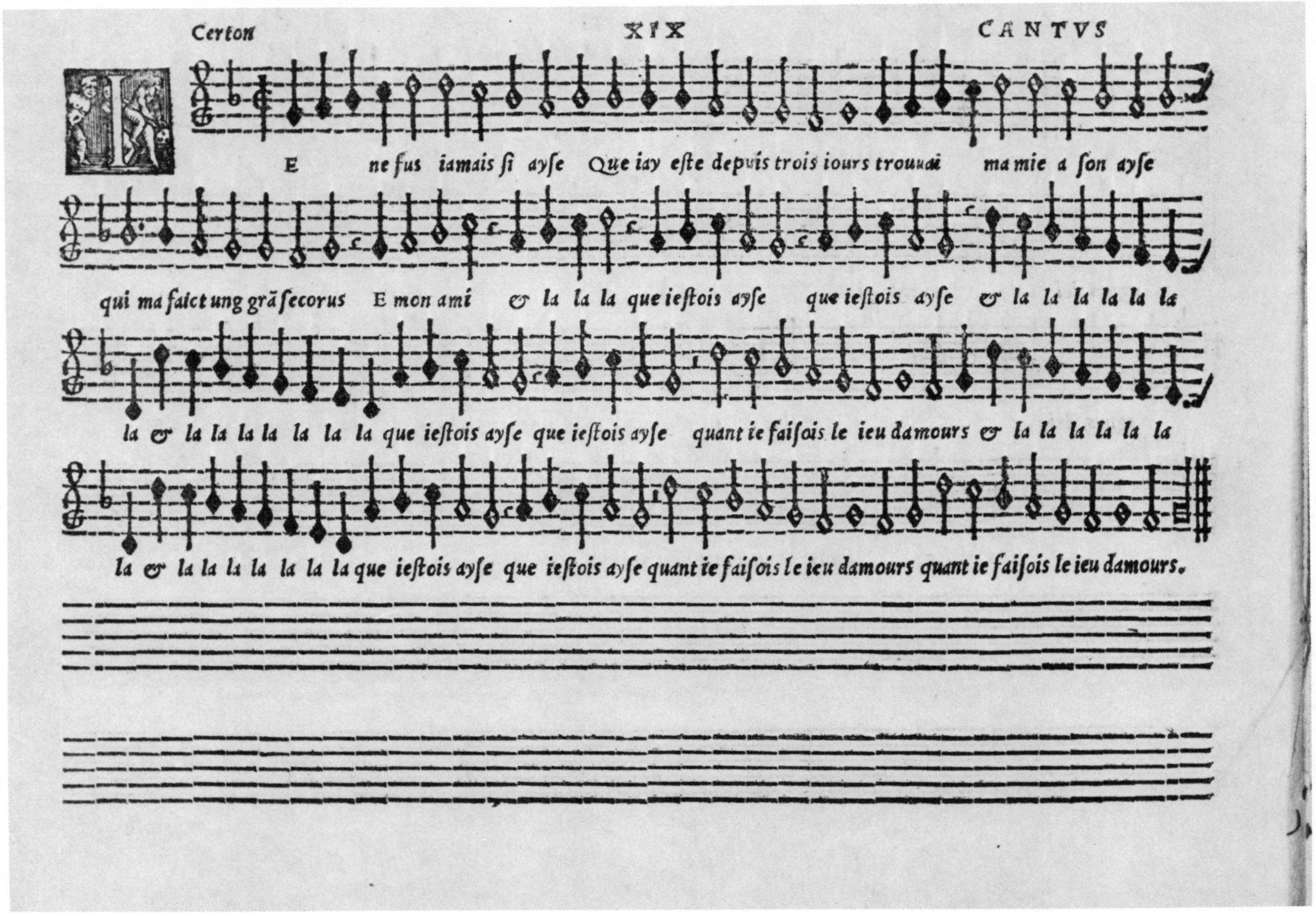
Certon
XIX
CANTVS
E ne fus iamais ſi ayſe Que iay eſte depuis trois iours trouuai ma mie a ſon ayſe
qui ma faict ung grā ſecorus E mon ami & la la la que ieſtois ayſe que ieſtois ayſe & la la la la la la
la & la la la la la la la que ieſtois ayſe que ieſtois ayſe quant ie faiſois le ieu damours & la la la la la la
la & la la la la la la la que ieſtois ayſe que ieſtois ayſe quant ie faiſois le ieu damours quant ie faiſois le ieu damours.

Plate IV. *Primo libro di madrigali d'Archadelt*. Venetiis: Antonium Gardane, 1543. Cantus partbook. Page 19. (Courtesy of the Österreichische Nationalbibliothek).

# THREE-PART CHANSONS
# PRINTED BY GARDANE (1541[13])

# [1] Jennette, Marion se vont jouer

[Anonymous]

Cantus
Tenor
Bassus
Jen- net- te, Ma- ri- on se vont jou- er, ⟨Jen-
Jen- net- te, Ma- ri-
Jen- net- te, Ma- ri- on se vont
5
- net- te, Ma- ri- on se vont jou- er⟩ aux
- on, Jen- net- te, Ma- ri- on se vont jou- er aux
jou- er, ⟨Jen- net- te, Ma- ri- on se vont jou- - er⟩ aux
10
champs, El- le ont pleu- mé leur con poil a poil, poil a
champs, El- le ont pleu- mé leur con, ⟨El- le ont pleu-mé leur con⟩ poil a
champs, El- le ont pleu-mé leur con, El- le ont pleu-mé leur con

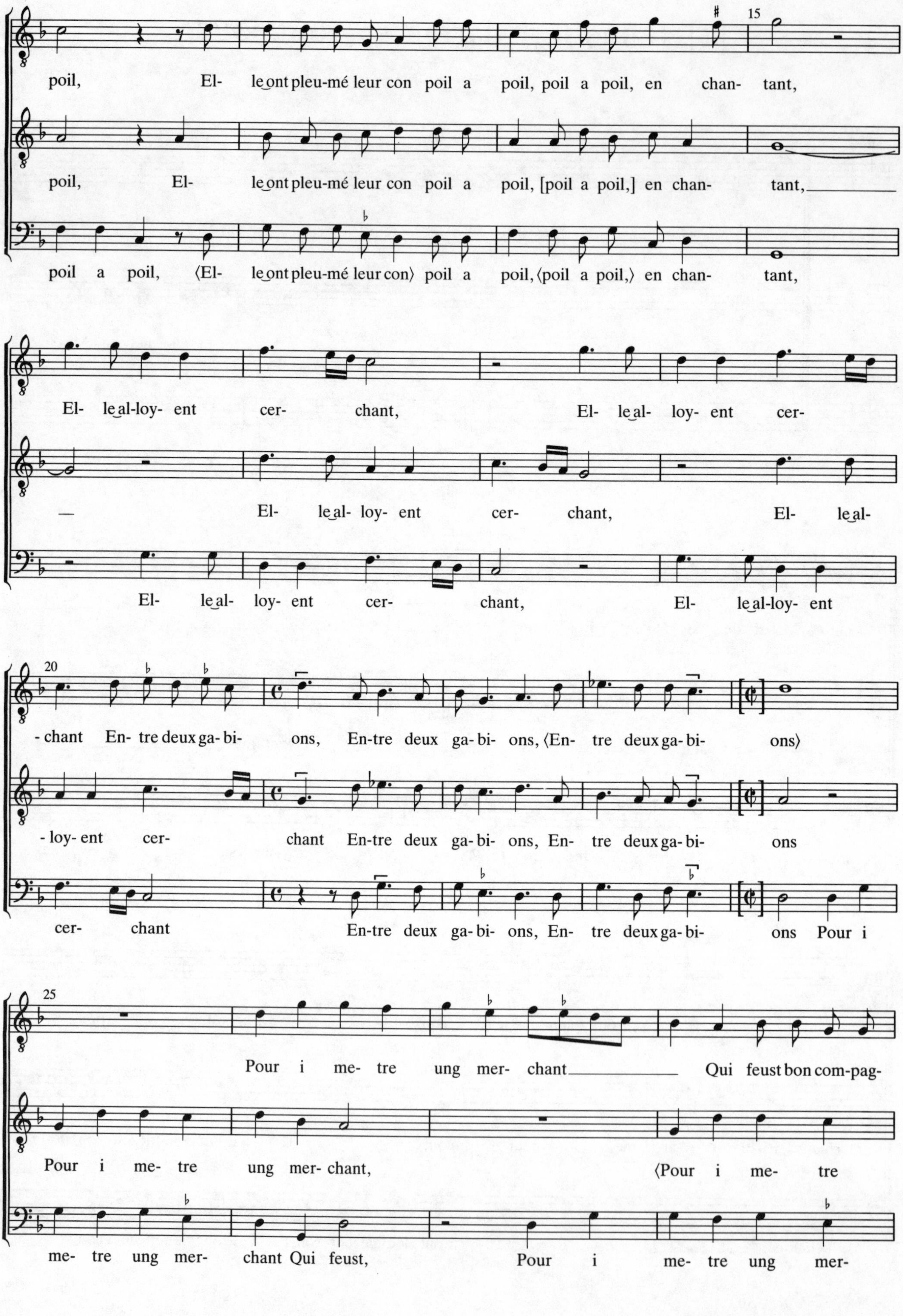
15
poil, El- le͜ ont pleu-mé leur con poil a poil, poil a poil, en chan- tant,
poil, El- le͜ ont pleu-mé leur con poil a poil, [poil a poil,] en chan- tant,
poil a poil, ⟨El- le͜ ont pleu-mé leur con⟩ poil a poil, ⟨poil a poil,⟩ en chan- tant,
El- le͜ al-loy- ent cer- chant, El- le͜ al- loy- ent cer-
El- le͜ al- loy- ent cer- chant, El- le͜ al-
El- le͜ al- loy- ent cer- chant, El- le͜ al-loy- ent
20
-chant En- tre deux ga- bi- ons, En-tre deux ga- bi- ons, ⟨En- tre deux ga- bi- ons⟩
-loy- ent cer- chant En-tre deux ga- bi- ons, En- tre deux ga- bi- ons
cer- chant En-tre deux ga- bi- ons, En- tre deux ga- bi- ons Pour i
25
Pour i me- tre ung mer- chant Qui feust bon com-pag-
Pour i me- tre ung mer- chant, ⟨Pour i me- tre
me- tre ung mer- chant Qui feust, Pour i me- tre ung mer-

30
- non, bon, bon, ⟨Qui feust bon com-pag-non⟩ Et bon be- la- ri- bon, bon, bon,
ung mer-chant⟩ Qui feust bon com-pag- non Et bon be- la- ri- bon, bon, bon,
- chant Qui feust bon com-pag- non Et bon be- la- ri- bon, bon, bon,
35
Pour i me- tre ung mer- chant Qui feust, qui feust bon com-pag- non Et bon be- la- ri-
Pour i me- tre ung mer- chant Qui feust bon com-pag- non Et bon be- la- ri-
Pour i me- tre ung mer- chant Qui feust, ⟨qui feust⟩ bon com-pag- non Et bon be- la- ri-
- bon, Et bon be- la- ri- bon, bon, bon, bon [bon,] Et bon be- la- ri- bon, bon, bon, bon, bon.
- bon, bon.
- bon, Et bon be- la- ri- bon, bon, bon, bon, bon, Et bon be- la- ri- bon, bon, bon.

# [2] Regretz, soucy et peine

[Guillaume Le Heurteur]

Cantus
Re- gretz, sou- cy et pei- ne M'ont fait de
Tenor
Re- gretz, sou-
Bassus
Re- gretz, sou- cy et pei- ne M'ont
5
vil- lains tours, Si pi- tyé n'est sou- dai- ne, Tost
-cy et pei- - ne M'ont fait de vil- lains tours,
fait de vil- lains tours, Si pi- tyé n'est sou-
10
fi- ni- ray mes jours, ⟨Si pi- tyé n'est sou-
Si pi- tyé n'est sou- dai- - ne, Tost fi- ni- ray mes
-dai- ne, Tost fi- ni- ray mes jours, Si pi- tyé n'est sou- dai-

15
-dai- ne, Tost fi- ni- ray mes jours;⟩ Hel-las, ce
jours, ⟨Tost fi- ni- ray mes jours;⟩ Hel- las, ce sont a- mours
- ne, Tost fi- ni- ray mes jours; Hel-las, ce sont a-mours Qui
20
sont a- mours Qui me font tout ce- - cy,
Qui me font tout ce- - cy, J'ay bruit et re- no-
me font tout ce- cy, [tout ce- cy,] J'ay bruit et re- no- mé-
25
J'ay bruit et re- no- mé- - e D'a- voir nou- vel a- my,
-mé- e D'a- voir nou- vel a- - my, J'ay bruit et re- no-
-e D'a- voir nou- vel a- my, ⟨D'a- voir nou- vel a- my,⟩ J'ay
30
J'ay bruit et re- no- mé- - e D'a- voir nou- vel a- my.
-mé- e D'a- voir nou- vel a- - my.
bruit et re- no- mé- e D'a- voir nou- vel a- my.

# [3] C'est une dure despartie

[Claudin de Sermisy]

Cantus
C'est u- ne du- re des- par- ti-
Tenor
C'est u- ne du- re des-
Bassus
C'est u- ne du- re des- par- ti- e, des- par-
5
- e De ce- luy ou j'ay mis mon cueur, Dont
-par- ti- e De ce- luy ou j'ay mis mon
-ti- e De ce- luy ou j'ay mis mon cueur, [j'ay mis mon
10
m'en i- ray u- ser ma vi- - e A l'her- mi- ta- ge de
cueur, Dont m'en i- ray u- ser ma vi- e A l'her-mi-
cueur,] Dont m'en i- ray u- ser ma vi- e A l'her-mi- ta- ge
15
lan-gueur; Et tous les jours au ma- ti- -
-ta- ge de lan- gueur; Et tous les jours au
de lan- - gueur; Et tous les jours au ma- ti-

- net Je m'en i- ray chan- ter sur
ma- ti- net i- ray chan- ter sur
- net Je
la ver- du- re, Soubz le cou- vert d'ung buis- so-
la ver- du- re, Soubz le cou- vert d'ung buis-
m'en i- ray chan- ter sur la ver- du- re, Soubz le cou- vert
- net, La pei- - ne que pour luy je en- du-
- so- - net, La pei- - ne que pour luy je en- du-
d'ung buis- so- net, La pei- ne que pour luy je en- du-
- re, La pei- - ne que pour luy je en- du- - re.
- - re, La pei- ne que pour luy je en- du- re.
- re, La pei- ne que pour luy je en- du- - re.

# [4] Je ne fais rien que requérir

[Clément Marot] [Claudin de Sermisy]

Cantus
Tenor
Bassus
Je ne fais rien que re- qué- rir Sans ac- qué-
Je ne fais rien que re- qué- - rir
Je ne fais rien que re- qué- rir Sans ac- qué- rir, [Sans
5
- rir, [Sans ac- qué- rir] Le don d'a- mou-
Sans ac- qué- - rir Le don d'a- mou-
ac- qué- rir] Le don d'a- mou- reu- se ly- es- se
10
- reu- se ly- - es- se. Las, ma mais- tres-
- reu- se ly- - es- se. Las, ma mais- tres-
⟨d'a- mou- reu- se ly- es- se.⟩ Las, ma mais-

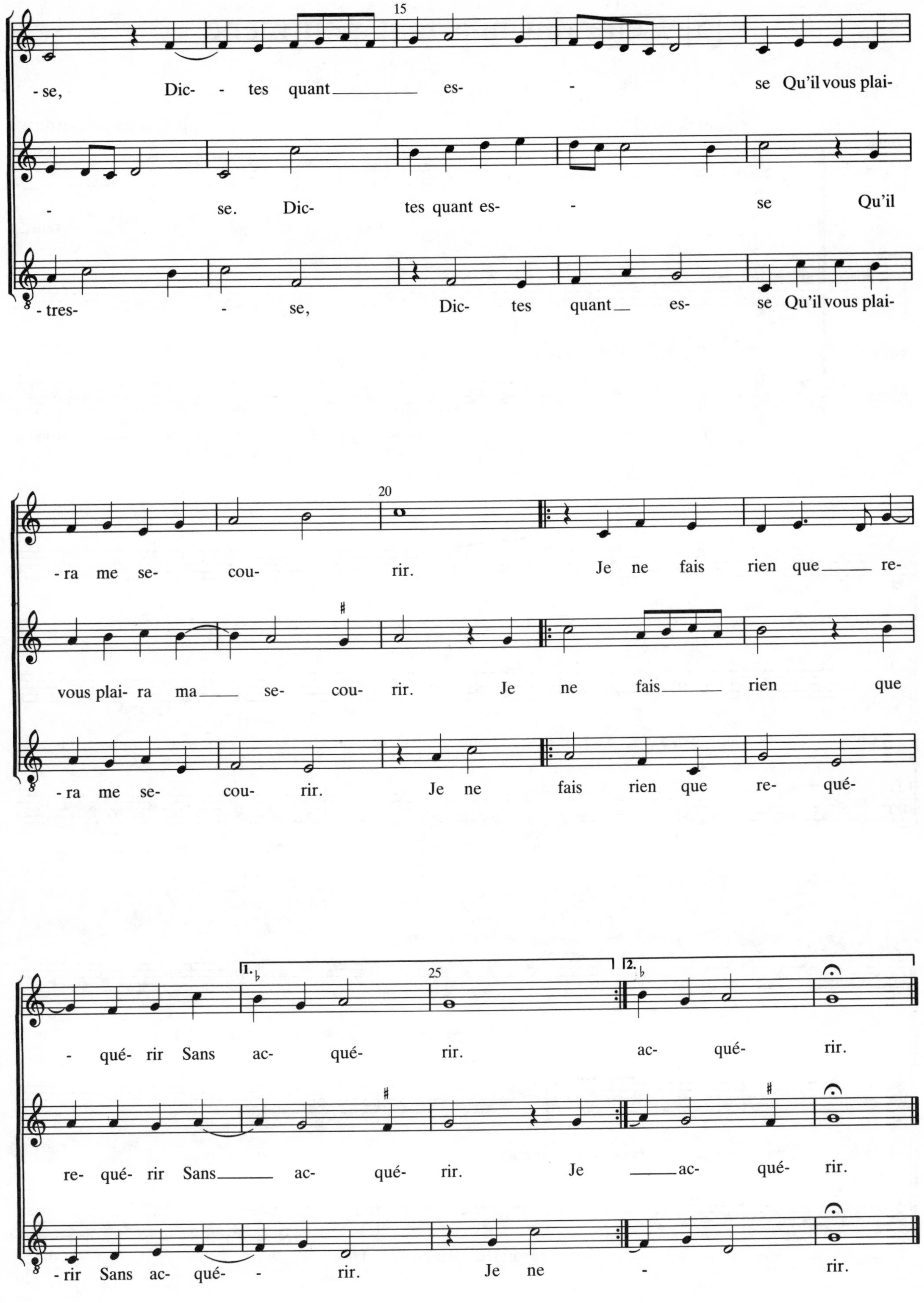
- se, Dic- - tes quant es- - se Qu'il vous plai-
- se. Dic- tes quant es- - se Qu'il
- tres- - se, Dic- tes quant es- se Qu'il vous plai-
- ra me se- cou- rir. Je ne fais rien que re-
vous plai- ra ma se- cou- rir. Je ne fais rien que
- ra me se- cou- rir. Je ne fais rien que re- qué-
- qué- rir Sans ac- qué- rir. ac- qué- rir.
re- qué- rir Sans ac- qué- rir. Je ac- qué- rir.
- rir Sans ac- qué- - rir. Je ne - rir.

# [5] Celle qui m'a tant pourmené

[Clément Marot] [Claudin de Sermisy]

Cantus
Tenor
Bassus
Cel- le qui m'a tant
Cel- le qui m'a tant pour- me- né, [tant
5
pour- me- né A eu pi- tié de
Cel- le qui m'a tant pour- me- né A eu pi-
pour- me- né] A eu pi- tié de ma
10
ma lan- - gueur; De- dans son jar- din
- tié de ma lan- gueur;
lan- - gueur; De- dans son jar- - din

15
— m'a me- né, [m'a me- né] Ou tous ar- bres sont
De- dans son jar- din m'a me- né Ou tous ar-
m'a me- né Ou tous ar- bres sont
20
en vi- - gueur, ⟨Ou tous ar- bres sont
- bres sont en vi- gueur, ⟨Ou tous ar-
en vi- - gueur,
25
[o = o·]
en vi- - gueur;⟩ A- donc- ques
- bres sont en vi- - gueur;⟩ A- donc- ques
⟨Ou tous ar- bres sont en vi- - gueur;⟩ A- donc- ques
30
[o· = o]
meu- sa sa ri- gueur. Si je la bai-se, el-le m'a- - col-
meu- sa sa ri- gueur. Si je la bai- se, el- le m'a-
meu- sa sa ri- gueur. Si je la bai-se, el-le m'a- col- le,

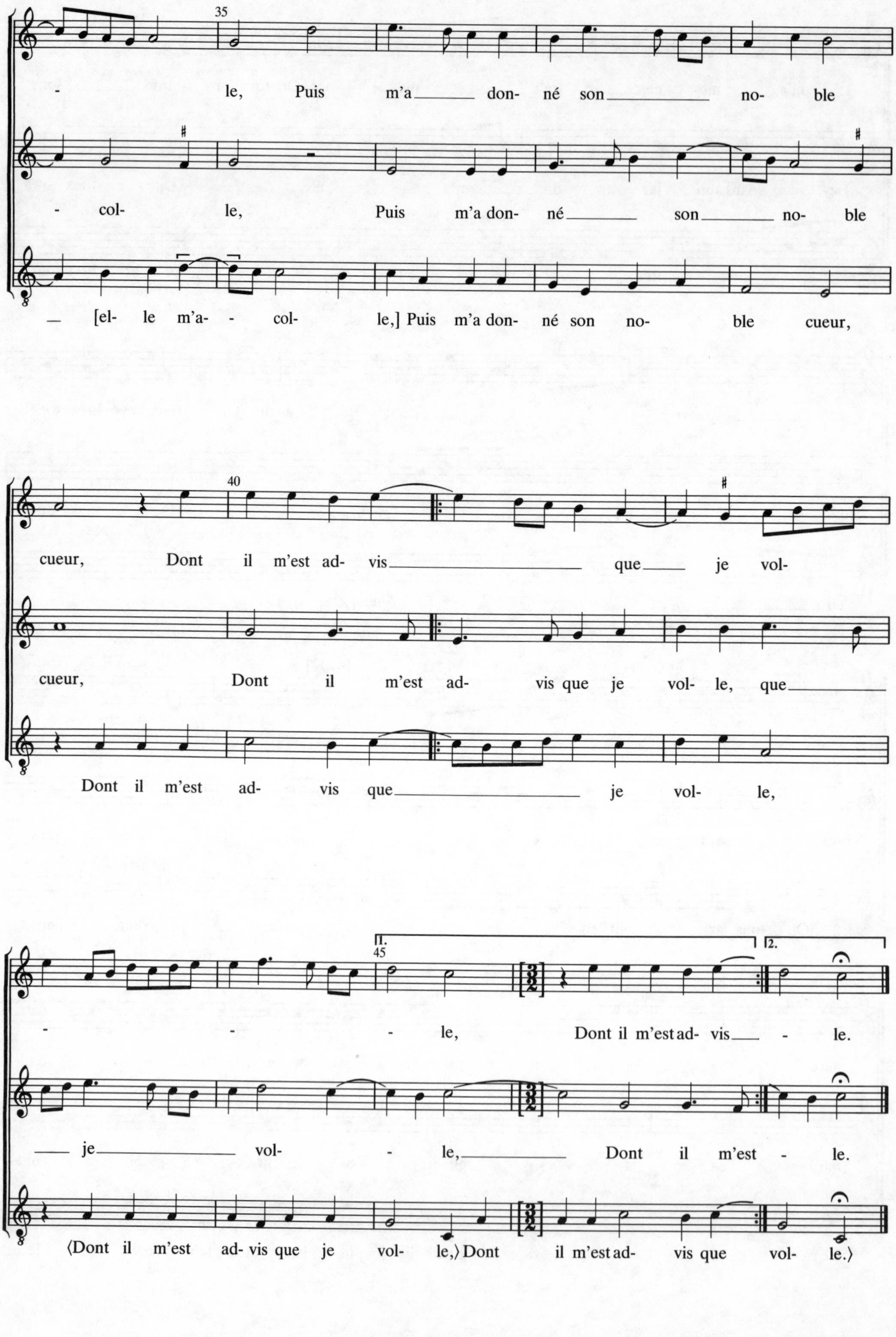
35
- le, Puis m'a don- né son no- ble
- col- le, Puis m'a don- né son no- ble
[el- le m'a- - col- le,] Puis m'a don- né son no- ble cueur,
40
cueur, Dont il m'est ad- vis que je vol-
cueur, Dont il m'est ad- vis que je vol- le, que
Dont il m'est ad- vis que je vol- le,
1.
45
2.
- - - le, Dont il m'est ad- vis - le.
je vol- - le, Dont il m'est - le.
⟨Dont il m'est ad- vis que je vol- le,⟩ Dont il m'est ad- vis que vol- le.⟩

# [6] Au pres de vous secretement demeure

[Claudin de Sermisy]

Cantus
Tenor
Bassus
Au pres de vous
Au pres de
Au pres de vous se-
5
se- cre- te- ment de- meu- re, se- cre- te- ment de-
vous se- cre- te- ment de- meu- re, se- cre- te-
- cre- te-ment de- meu- re, se- cre- te-ment de- meu-
10
- - meu- re Mon po- vre cueur sans que nul
- ment de- - meu- re Mon po- vre cueur sans que nul le
- - - re Mon po- vre cueur sans que nul
15
le con- for- - - te, Et si lan- guis
con-for- te, Et si lan- guis
le con- for- - te, le con- for- te, Et si lan- guis

20
pour la dou-leur qui por- - te,
pour la dou-leur qui por- - -
pour la dou- leur qui por- te,
25
Puis que vou- lés qu'en
- te, Puis que vou- lés
Puis que vou- - lés qu'en ce tour-ment il
30
ce tour- ment il meu- re, qu'en ce tour- ment il
qu'en ce tour- ment il meu- re, il meu-
meu- re, qu'en ce tour-ment il meu-
35
meu- re, Puis re.
- - - - re, re.
- - re, Puis re.
1.
2.

# [7] Tant est gentil, plaisant et gracieulx

[Anonymous]

Cantus
Tant est gen- til,
Tenor
Tant est gen- til,
Bassus
Tant est gen- til ⟨gen-
— plai- - sant et gra- - ci-
— plai- sant et gra- ci- -
- til,⟩ plai- - sant et gra- - ci- eulx,
- eulx, Plain de tous biens plus que
- eulx, Plain de tous biens plus que rien
Plain de tous biens

15
rien soubz les cieulx; Le
soubz les cieulx;
plus que rien soubz les
20
cueur rem- ply d'a- mour vray et per- faict, ⟨vray et
Le cueur rem- ply d'a- mour vray et per-
cieulx; Le cueur rem- ply d'a- mour vray
25
per- faict⟩ Que par hon- neur
faict Que par hon- neur, [que par
et per- faict Que par hon-
30
ne dé- sy- re en
hon- neur] ne dé- sy- re en son
neur ne dé- sy-

35
son faict
faict, ⟨en son faict⟩ Fors
- re en son faict Fors
40
Fors bien ay- mer et ha- yr vi- -
bien ay- mer, fors bien ay- mer et ha- yr vi-
bien ay- mer et ha- yr vi- - ci-
- - - ci- eulx.
- ci- eulx, vi- - ci- - eulx.
- eulx, vi- ci- eulx.

# [8] Amour, Amour, tu es par trop cruelle

[Anonymous]

Cantus
Tenor
Bassus
A- mour, A- mour, tu es par trop cru- el-
A- mour, A- mour, tu es par trop cru- el-
A- mour, A- mour, tu es par trop cru- el-
5
- le. Quant tes a- - mantz qui ne pen-
- le. Quant tes a- mantz qui ne pen-
- le. Quant tes a- - mantz qui ne pen-
10
- sent que a bien, Tu n'en sçays rien; mais
- sent que a bien, Tu n'en sçays rien; mais
- sent que a bien, Tu n'en sçays rien; mais

15
mon cueur le sçaict bien, [le sçaict bien,] Se͜ a-
mon cueur le sçaict bien, ⟨le sçaict bien,⟩ Se͜ a-
mon cueur le sçaict bien, Se͜ a-
20
-mour me prent, c'est cho- se na- - tu- rel-
-mour me prent, c'est cho- se na- - tu-
-mour me prent, c'est cho- se na- - tu- rel-
25
- le, c'est cho- se na- tu- - rel- le.
-rel- le, c'est cho- se na- tu- - rel- le.
- le, c'est cho- se na- tu- rel- le.

# [9] Mauldicte soit la mondaine richesse

[Clément Marot] [Cosson]

Cantus
Tenor
Bassus
Maul- dic- te soit la mon- dai- ne ri- - ches-
Maul- dic- te soit la mon- dai- ne ri-
Maul- dic- te soit la
5
- - se Qui m'a os- té ma da-
- ches- - se
mon- dai- ne ri- ches- - se Qui m'a os- té ma
10
- me et ma mais- tres- - - se,
Qui m'a os- té ma da- me et ma mais- tres- - se, Las,
da- me, qui m'a os- té ma da- me et ma mais- tres- se,
15
Las, par ver- tu j'ay son a- mi- tié a-
par ver- - tu j'ay son a- mi- tié a- qui-
Las, par ver- tu j'ay son a- mi- - tié a-

20
-qui- se, Mais par ri- ches- se, mais par ri- ches- se‿ung aul-
- se, Mais par ri- ches- se‿ung
-qui- se, Mais par ri- ches- se ⟨mais par ri- ches-
25
-tre l'a con- qui- - - se; Ver- tu n'a
aul- tre l'a con- - qui- - se; Ver- tu n'a pas en
-se⟩ung aul- tre l'a con- qui- se, l'a con- qui- se; Ver- tu n'a
30
pas en a- - mour grant prou- - es- se, Ver-
a- mour grant prou- - es- se, Ver- tu n'a pas,
pas en a- mour grant prou- es- se, grant prou- es- se, Ver- tu n'a
35
-tu n'a pas, ver-tu n'a pas en a- mour grant prou-es- se.
ver- tu n'a pas en a- mour grant prou- - es- se.
pas en a- mour grant prou- es- se, en a- mour grant prou- es- se.

# [10] La loy d'amours est tant inique et dure

[Anonymous]

Cantus
Tenor
Bassus
La loy d'a-mours, ⟨la loy d'a- mours⟩ est
La loy d'a- mours, ⟨la loy d'a-mours,⟩ la loy d'a-
La loy d'a- mours, ⟨la loy d'a-mours⟩
5
tant i- ni- - que et du- re, La
-mours est tant i- ni- que et du- re,
est tant i- ni- que et du- re, La pas- si-
10
pas- si- on si doul- ce sans me- su-
La pas- si- on si doul- ce sans me-
-on si doul- ce sans me- su- re Qu'el-
15
- re Qu'el- le me sfor- se suy-
- su- re Qu'el- le me sfor- se suy- vre jus-
-le me sfor- se, ⟨qu'el- le me sfor- se⟩ suy- vre jus-

20
- vre jus- que‿a - la mort, Que chas-cun jour, ⟨que chas-
- que‿a la mort, Que chas- cun jour, ⟨que chas- cun jour⟩
- que‿a la mort, Que chas-cun jour, ⟨que chas-cun
25
- cun jour⟩ me faict - in- ju- re‿et tort
me faict in- ju- re‿et tort Et suis con-
jour⟩ me faict in- ju- re‿et tort Et suis con-
30
Et suis con- tent du mal-heur que j'en- du- - re,
- tent, ⟨et suis con- tent⟩ du mal-heur que j'en- du- re, Et suis con-
- tent, ⟨et suis con- tent⟩ du mal-heur que j'en- du- re, Et suis con-
Et suis con- tent du mal- heur que j'en- du- - re.
- tent, ⟨et suis con- tent⟩ du mal- heur que j'en- du- re.
- tent, ⟨et suis con- tent⟩ du mal- heur que j'en- du- re.

# [11] Contre raison vous m'estes fort estrange

[Claudin de Sermisy]

Cantus
Tenor
Bassus
Con- tre rai- son vous m'es- tes
Con- tre rai- son vous
Con- - tre rai- son vous
5
fort es- tran- - ge. E- se bien
m'es-tes fort es- tran- ge. E- se bien faict;
m'es-tes fort es- - tran- ge. E- se bien faict; en au- res
10
faict; en au- res vous lou- en- - - ge, D'ain-
en au- - res vous lou- en- - ge,
vous lou- en- ge [en au- res vous lou- en- ge,] D'ain-sy m'a-
15
- sy m'a-voir sou- dain dés- hé- ri- -
D'ain- sy m'a- voir sou- dain dés- - hé- ri-
- voir sou- dain dés- - hé- ri- - té

té De vos- tre‿a- mour sans l'a- voir
- té De vos- tre‿a- mour sans l'a- voir mé- ri-
De vos- tre‿a- mour sans l'a- voir mé- ri-
mé- ri- té? Vous faict il mal se‿a vous ser- vir, ⟨se‿a vous ser-
- té? Vous faict il mal se‿a vous
- té? Vous faict il mal se‿a vous ser- vir me ren-
- vir⟩ me ren- - - ge, se‿a
ser- vir me ren- - ge? Vous faict il
- ge, [se‿a vous ser- vir me ren- ge?] Vous faict il
vous ser- vir, ⟨se‿a vous ser- vir⟩ me ren- ge?
mal se‿a vous ser- vir me ren- - ge?
mal se‿a vous ser- vir me ren- ge [ser- vir me ren- ge?]

# [12] Le cueur de vous ma présence désire

[Clément Marot] [Anonymous]

Cantus
Tenor
Bassus
Le cueur de vous ma
Le cueur de vous ma pré- sen- ce dé- si-
Le cueur de vous ma pré-sen- ce dé- si-
5
pré- sen- ce dé- - si- re, Mais pour
-re, Mais pour le mieulx bel- le je me re- ti- re,
- re, Mais pour le mieulx, ⟨mais
10
le mieulx bel- le je me re- - ti- re,
⟨Mais pour le mieulx bel- le je me re- ti- re,⟩ Car sans
pour le mieulx⟩ bel- le je me re- ti- re, Car

Car sans a- voir aul- tre con- - ten- te- ment Je
a- voir aul- tre con- ten- te- ment Je ne pour-roys, je
sans a- voir aul- tre con- ten- te- ment Je ne pour-roys,
ne pour- roys ser- vir si lon-gue- ment. Ve-
ne pour-roys ser- vir si lon- - gue- ment. Ve-nons au
je ne pour- roys ser- - vir si lon- gue- - ment.
-nons au point, ve- nons au point, au point qu'on
point, au point qu'on ne o- se di- re, Ve- nons au
Ve- nons au point, au point qu'on ne o- se di-
ne o- se di- - - re. Ve- re.
point, au point qu'on ne o- se di- re. Ve-nons au re.
- re, ⟨qu'on ne o- se di- re.⟩ re.⟩

# [13] J'ay le désir content et le faict resolu

[Claude Chappuys?] [Claudin de Sermisy]

Cantus
J'ay le dé- sir con- tent
Tenor
J'ay le dé- sir con- tent
Bassus
J'ay le dé- sir con- tent et
et le faict re- - so- lu. J'ay le sça-
et le faict re- so- - lu.
le faict re- - so- lu. J'ay
-voir cer- tain car
J'ay le sça- voir cer- tain car A- mour
le sça- voir cer- tain car A- mour l'a

15
A- mour l'a vou- lu Par quoy je tiens mon
l'a vou- - lu Par quoy je tiens mon
vou- lu Par quoy je tiens mon bien de
20
bien de l'heu- reu-se pen- - sé- e En tres bien le gar-
bien de l'heu- reu- se pen- sé- e En tres bien le gar-
l'heu- reu- - se pen- sé- e En tres bien le gar-
25
- dant que ne soit of- fen- sé- e, Dont pour ma li- ber-
- dant que ne soit of- - fen- sé- e, Dont pour ma
- dant que ne soit of- fen- sé- e, Dont pour ma li- ber-
30
- té a al- trui m'a- - ban- don- ne Que le moins
li- ber- té a al- trui m'a- - ban- don- - - ne
- té a al- trui m'a- ban- don- ne Que

35
de son plus trop
Que le moins de son plus trop myeulx que
le moins de son plus trop myeulx que moy
1.
2.
40
myeulx que moy me don- ne, Que le moins don- ne.
moy me don- - ne, don- ne.
me don- ne, Que don- ne.

# [14] Grace et vertu, bonté, beaulté, noblesse

[Guillaume Le Heurteur]

Cantus
Gra- ce‿et ver- tu, bon- té, beaul- té, bon-
Tenor
Gra- ce‿et ver- tu, bon- té, beaul-
Bassus
Gra- ce‿et ver- tu, bon- té, beaul- té, no-

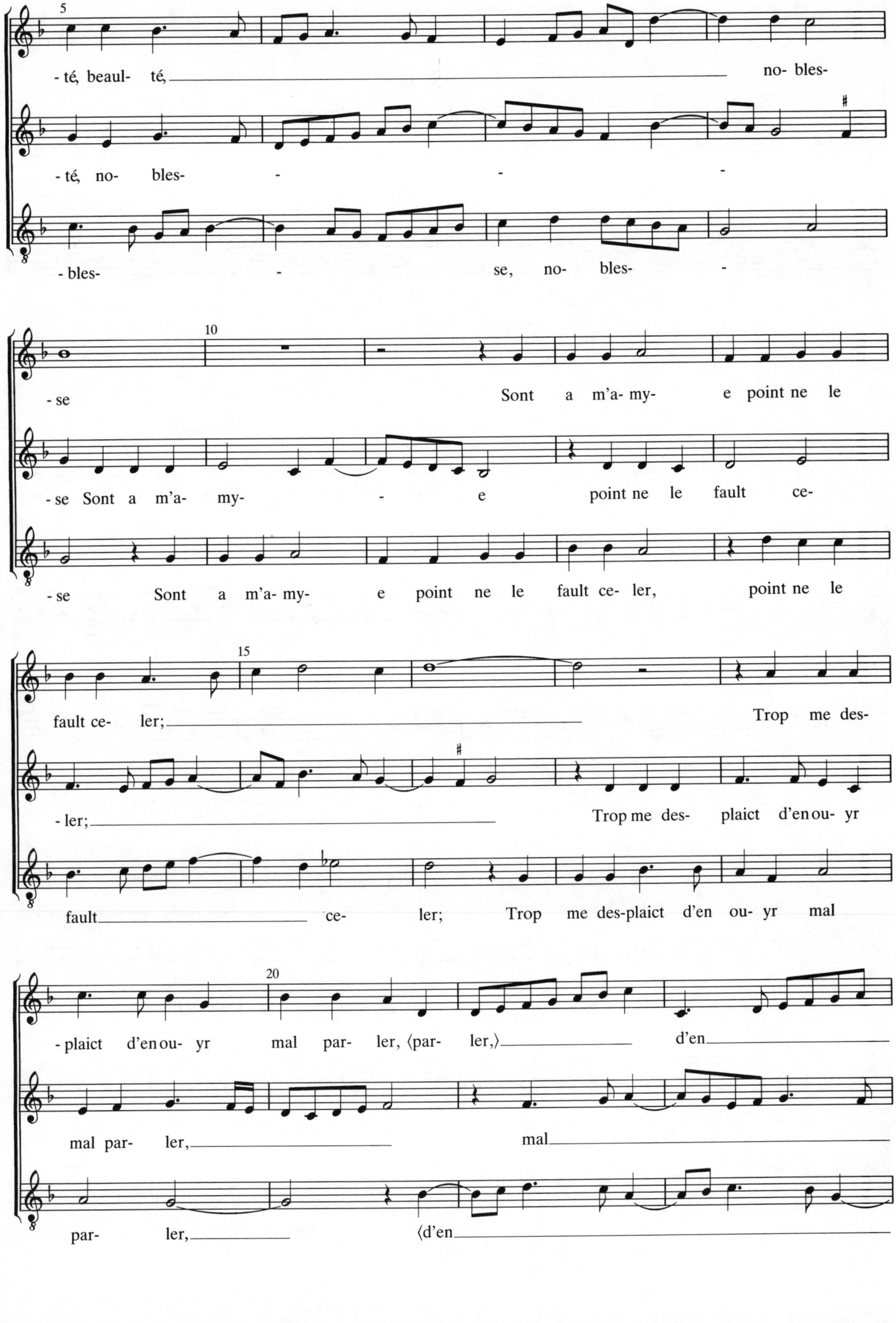
-té, beaul- té, no- bles-
-té, no- bles- - - -
-bles- - se, no- bles- -
-se Sont a m'a- my- e point ne le
-se Sont a m'a- my- - e point ne le fault ce-
-se Sont a m'a- my- e point ne le fault ce- ler, point ne le
fault ce- ler; Trop me des-
-ler; Trop me des- plaict d'en ou- yr
fault ce- ler; Trop me des-plaict d'en ou- yr mal
-plaict d'en ou- yr mal par- ler, ⟨par- ler,⟩ d'en
mal par- ler, mal
par- ler, ⟨d'en

ou- yr mal par- - ler, Je hay cel- luy qui l'hon-neur
par- - ler, Je hay cel-
ou- yr mal par- ler,⟩ Je hay cel- luy
d'el- le, qui l'hon-neur d'el- - le
-luy qui l'hon-neur d'el- le bles- -
qui l'hon-neur d'el- le bles- - -
bles- - se, Je hay cel- - se.
- - - se, - se.
- - se, Je hay cel- luy - se.
1.
2.

# [15] Amour, me voyant sans tristesse

[Clément Marot]

[Gosse]

Cantus
Tenor
Bassus
A- mour, me voy- ant sans tris- tes- - se
A- mour, me voy- ant sans tris- tes- - se
A- mour, me voy- ant sans tris- tes- se Et
Et de le ser- vir des- gou- té, M'a
Et de le ser- vir des- gou- - té, M'a
de le ser-vir des- gou- té, ⟨le ser- vir des- gou- té,⟩ M'a
dict que je feis- se u- ne mais- - tres- se
dict que je feis- - se u- ne mais- tres- se Et
dict que je feis- se u- ne mais- tres- se Et qu'il se-
Et qu'il se- roit de mon cos- té. A-
qu'il se- roit de mon cos- - té. A- pres l'a- voir
- roit de mon cos- té, ⟨se- roit de mon cos- té.⟩ A- pres l'a-

-pres l'a- voir bien es- - cou- té, J'en ay faict
bien es- cou- té, J'en ay faict u-
-voir bien es- cou- té, J'en ay faict u- ne a
u- ne a ma plai- san- - ce; Et ne me suis point mes- con-
- ne a ma plai- san- ce; Et ne me suis point
ma plai- san- ce; Et ne me suis point mes-
- té, C'est
mes- con- - té, C'est bien la plus bel- le
- con- té, C'est bien la plus bel- le,
bien la plus bel- le de Fran- ce, Et ne me ce.
de Fran- - - ce, Et ne me ce.
c'est bien la plus bel- le de Fran- ce, Et ne me ce.

# [16] Hellas, je suis marry de ces maulditz jaleux

[Antoine de Févin]

Cantus
Hel- las, je suis mar- - ry, hel- las,
Tenor
Hel- las, je suis mar- ry, hel- las,
Bassus
Hel- las, je suis mar- ry, hel- las,
hel- las, de ces maul-ditz ja- - leux
je suis mar- ry de ces maul- ditz ja- leux
hel- las, je suis mar- ry de ces maul- ditz ja-
Qui ont sur moy, qui ont sur moy
Qui ont sur moy,
- leux Qui ont sur moy, qui ont sur moy si

15
si grant fan- te- - - sie,
[qui ont sur moy] si grant fan- te- - sie,
grant fan- te- sie, ⟨si grant fan- te- - sie,⟩
20
Leur fem-mes n'ont bon- ne heu- - re ne
Leur fem- mes n'ont, [leur fem-mes n'ont] bon- ne heu-
Leur fem-mes n'ont bon- ne heu- re
25
de- - - mye, Hel- las, il leur sem-
- re ne de- mye, Hel- las, il leur sem- bloit,
ne de- - mye, Hel- las, il leur sem-
30
- bloit, il leur sem- - bloit que je en fus- se a-
hel- las, il leur sem- bloit que je en
- bloit, [il leur sem- - bloit] que je en

35
- mou- - reulx, Hel- las, il leur sem-
fus- se a- mou- reulx, Hel- las, il leur sem- bloit,
fus- se a- mou- reulx, Hel- las, il leur sem-
40
- bloit, [il leur sem- - bloit] que je en fus- se a-
⟨hel- las, il leur sem- bloit⟩ que je en
- bloit, [il leur sem- - bloit] que je en
45
- mou- - reulx, a- - mou- - reulx.
fus- se a- mou- reulx, ⟨que je en fus- se a- mou- reulx.⟩
fus- se a- mou- reulx, a- - mou- reulx.

# [17] Quant je boy du vin claret tout tourne

[Guillaume Le Heurteur]

Cantus
Tenor
Bassus
Quant je boy du vin cla-
Quant je boy du vin cla- ret tout tour-
- ret tout tour- - -
Quant je boy du vin cla- ret tout tour- ne, ⟨Quant je
- ne, ⟨Quant je boy du vin cla- ret tout tour-
- ne, tout tour- - ne, Et quant je
boy du vin cla- ret⟩ tout tour- - ne, Quant
- ne,⟩ ⟨Quant je boy du vin cla- ret tout tour- ne,⟩
n'en boy point tout ne tour- ne point, ⟨Et quant je
je n'en boy point tout ne tour- ne point,
Et quant je n'en boy point tout

15
n'en boy point tout ne tour- ne
— ⟨Quant je n'en boy point tout ne tour- ne point,⟩
— ne tour- ne point, ⟨tout ne tour- ne point,⟩ Et quant n'ay
point,⟩ Et quant n'ay mail- le ne de- nier je
tout ne tour- ne point,
mail- le ne de- nier je ne boyt point, ⟨Et quant n'ay mail- le
20
ne boyt point, Ne bel- le fil- le‿a mon cou-cher tout
Et quant n'ay mail-le ne de-nier je ne boyt point,
ne de- nier je ne boyt point,⟩ Ne bel- le fil- le‿a mon cou-
25
ne tour- ne point, ⟨tout ne tour- ne
Ne bel- le fil- le‿a mon cou- cher tout ne tour- ne
- cher tout ne tour- - ne

30
point.〉 Et quant de ces vins blancs je boy Si ne sont
point. Et quant de ces vins blancs je boy Si ne sont
point. Et quant de ces vins blancs je boy Si ne sont d'An-jou ou
d'An- jou ou d'Ar- boys, point ne me tour- ne; Quant je
d'An- jou ou d'Ar- boys, point ne me tour- ne;
d'Ar- boys, point ne me tour- ne; Quant je boy du
35
boy du vin cla- ret [tout] tour- -
Quant je boy du vin cla- ret tout tour- ne,
vin cla- ret, 〈Quant je boy du vin cla- ret〉
40
- ne, tout tour- ne, tout tour- - ne.
〈Quant je boy du vin cla- ret tout tour- ne,〉 tout tour- - ne.
[tout tour- ne,] Quant je boy du vin cla- ret tout tour- ne.

# [18] Vignon, vignon, vignon, vignette

[Claudin de Sermisy]

Cantus
Tenor
Bassus
Vi- gnon, vi- gnon, vi- gnon, vi- gnet- te, Qui
Vi- gnon, vi-
Vi- gnon, vi- gnon, vi- gnon, vi- gnet- te, Qui te plan-
5
te plan- ta il fust preud-
-gnon, vi- gnon, vi- gnet- te, Qui te plan- ta il fust preud-
-ta il fust preud- hom. ⟨Qui te plan- ta il fust preud-
10
- - hom. Tu fuz cou- pé- e͜a la ser- pet- te,
-hom. Tu fuz cou- pé- - e͜a la ser- pet- -
-hom.⟩ Tu fuz cou- pé- e͜a la ser- pet- te, Vi-
15
Vi- gnon, vi- gnon, vi- gnon, vi- gnet- te, Il me sem-
- te, Vi- gnon, vi- gnon, vi- gnon, vi- gnet- te, Il
-gnon, vi- gnon, vi- gnon, vi- gnet- -

20
-ble ad- vis que j'a- lec- te Quant tu pas- ses mon gor- ge-
me sem- ble ad-vis que j'a- lec- - te Quant tu pas-
-te, Quant tu pas- ses per mon gor- ge-
25
-ron. Vi- gnon, vi- gnon,
-ses mon gor- ge- ron. Vi- gnon, vi- gnon,
-ron, [per mon gor- ge- ron.] Vi- gnon, vi-
30
⟨vi- gnon, vi- gnon,⟩ vi- gnon, vi- gnet- te,
vi- gnon, vi- gnet- te, Qui te plan- ta il
-gnon, vi- gnon, vi- gnet- - te, Qui te plan- ta,
1.
35
2.
Qui te plan- ta il fust preud- hom, Vi- gnon, vi- hom.
fust preud- hom, Vi- hom.
qui te plan- ta il fust preud- hom, hom.

# [19] Bastienne, Bastienne, vous avés changé d'amis

[Anonymous]

Cantus
Tenor
Bassus
Bas- ti- en- ne, Bas- ti- en- ne,
Bas- ti- en- ne, Bas- ti- en- ne, vous a-
Bas- ti- en- ne, Bas- ti- en- ne, vous a- vés chan- gé d'a- mis ⟨vous a-
5
vous a- vés chan- gé d'a- mis Vous a- vés lais- sé
- vés chan- gé d'a- mis Vous a- vés lais- sé Guil-lau- me
- vés chan- gé d'a- mis⟩ Vous a- vés lais- sé Guil-
10
Guil-lau- me, Guil- - lau- me, vous a- vés lais- sé Guil-lau- me
pour pren- dre pe- tit De- nis, ⟨vous a- vés lais- sé Guil-
- lau- me pour pren- - dre pe- tit De- nis, ⟨vous a- vés lais- sé

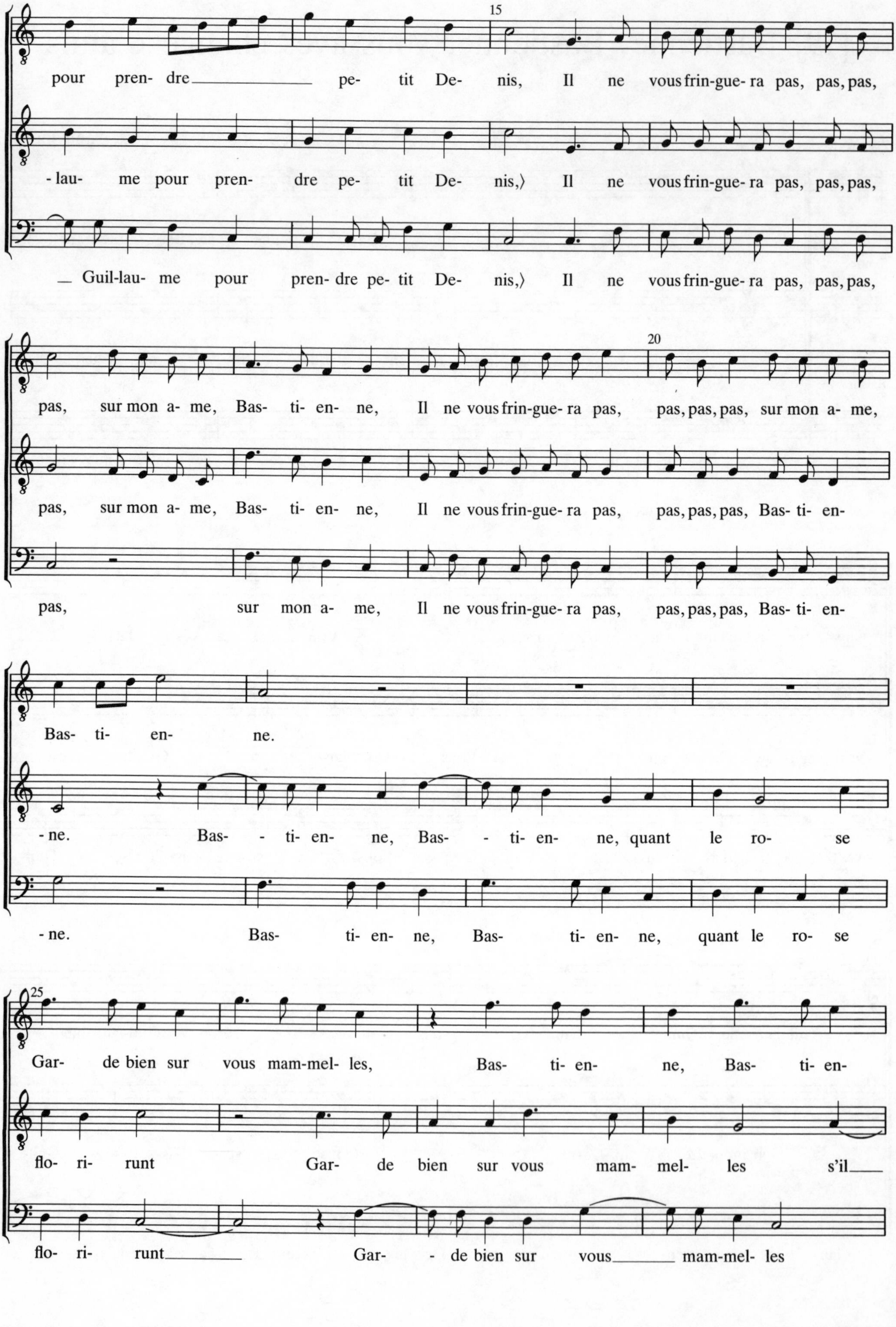
15
pour pren- dre pe- tit De- nis, Il ne vous frin-gue- ra pas, pas, pas,
-lau- me pour pren- dre pe- tit De- nis,⟩ Il ne vous frin-gue- ra pas, pas, pas,
Guil-lau- me pour pren- dre pe- tit De- nis,⟩ Il ne vous frin-gue- ra pas, pas, pas,
20
pas, sur mon a- me, Bas- ti- en- ne, Il ne vous frin-gue- ra pas, pas, pas, pas, sur mon a- me,
pas, sur mon a- me, Bas- ti- en- ne, Il ne vous frin-gue- ra pas, pas, pas, pas, Bas- ti- en-
pas, sur mon a- me, Il ne vous frin-gue- ra pas, pas, pas, pas, Bas- ti- en-
Bas- ti- en- ne.
-ne. Bas- ti- en- ne, Bas- ti- en- ne, quant le ro- se
-ne. Bas- ti- en- ne, Bas- ti- en- ne, quant le ro- se
25
Gar- de bien sur vous mam-mel- les, Bas- ti- en- ne, Bas- ti- en-
flo- ri- runt Gar- de bien sur vous mam- mel- les s'il
flo- ri- runt Gar- de bien sur vous mam-mel- les

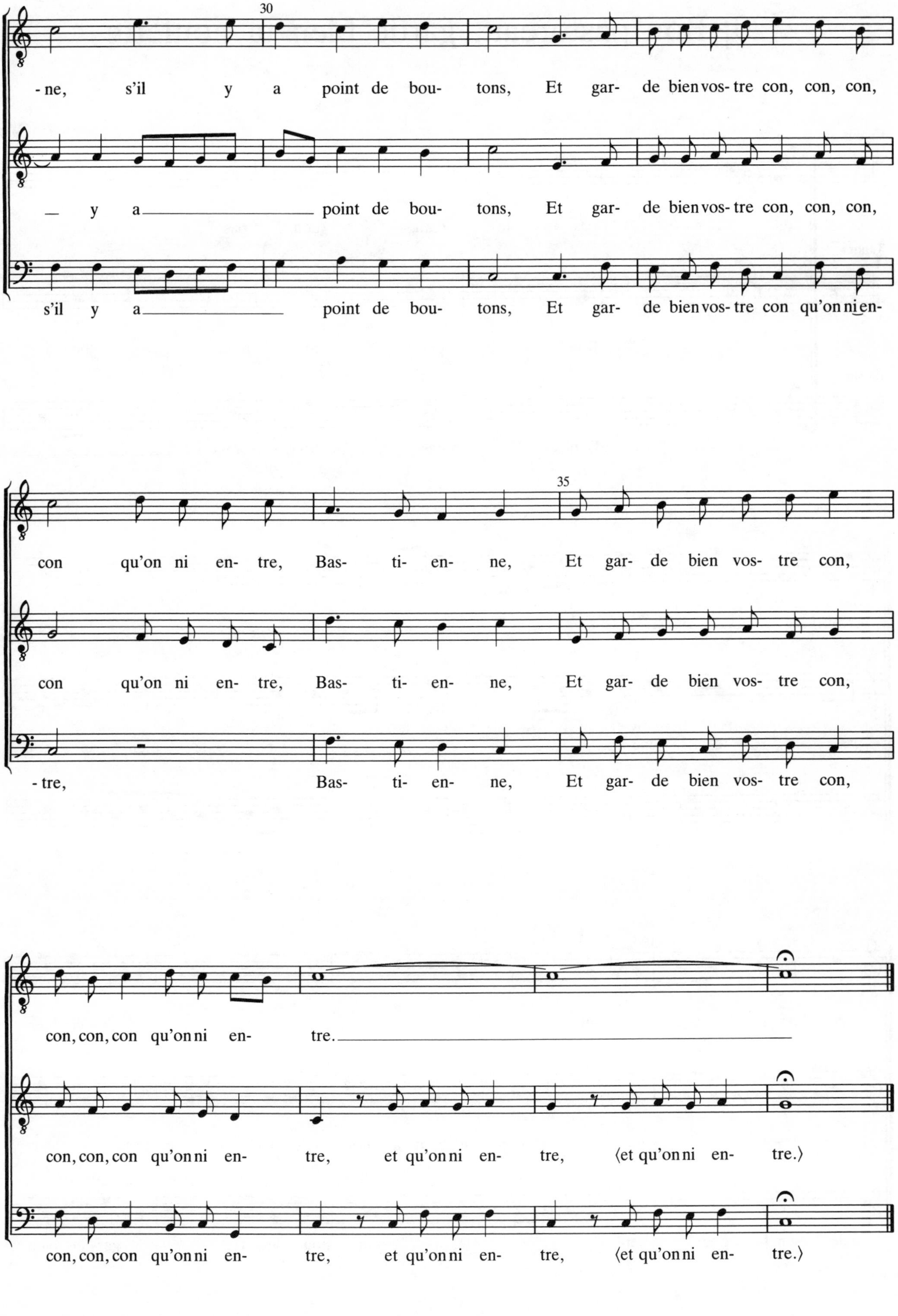
30
- ne, s'il y a point de bou- tons, Et gar- de bien vos- tre con, con, con,
— y a point de bou- tons, Et gar- de bien vos- tre con, con, con,
s'il y a point de bou- tons, Et gar- de bien vos- tre con qu'on ni en-
35
con qu'on ni en- tre, Bas- ti- en- ne, Et gar- de bien vos- tre con,
con qu'on ni en- tre, Bas- ti- en- ne, Et gar- de bien vos- tre con,
- tre, Bas- ti- en- ne, Et gar- de bien vos- tre con,
con, con, con qu'on ni en- tre.
con, con, con qu'on ni en- tre, et qu'on ni en- tre, ⟨et qu'on ni en- tre.⟩
con, con, con qu'on ni en- tre, et qu'on ni en- tre, ⟨et qu'on ni en- tre.⟩

# [20] Bon pastoreau, garde bien ta houlette

[Anonymous]

Cantus
Tenor
Bassus
Bon pas- to- reau, ⟨bon pas- to-
Bon pas- to- reau, ⟨bon
Bon pas- to- reau,
5
- reau,⟩ gar-
pas- to- reau,⟩ gar- de bien ta hou-
⟨bon pas- to- reau,⟩ gar-
10
- de bien ta hou- - let- - te, gar- de bien
- let- te, ⟨gar- de bien ta hou- - let- te,⟩ gar-
- de bien ta hou- let- te, ta hou- let- te, gar- de bien

ta hou- let- - te Pour dé- fen- dre des maul-ditz
-de bien ta hou- let- te Pour dé- fen-
ta hou- let- - - - te Pour dé-
loups ra- bis, Pour dé- fen- dre des maul-ditz loups ra-
-dre, ⟨pour dé- fen- dre⟩ des maul-ditz loups
-fen- dre des maul-ditz loups ra- - bis, des
-bis Tes doulx ag- neaulx, ⟨tes doulx ag- neaulx,⟩ ⟨tes
ra- - bis Tes doulx ag- neaulx, [tes doulx ag-
maul- ditz loups ra- bis Tes doulx ag- neaulx ⟨Tes doulx
doulx ag- - - neaulx,⟩ mou- tons beaulx et
-neaulx,] mou- tons beaulx et bre- bis,
ag- neaulx,⟩ mou- tons beaulx et bre-

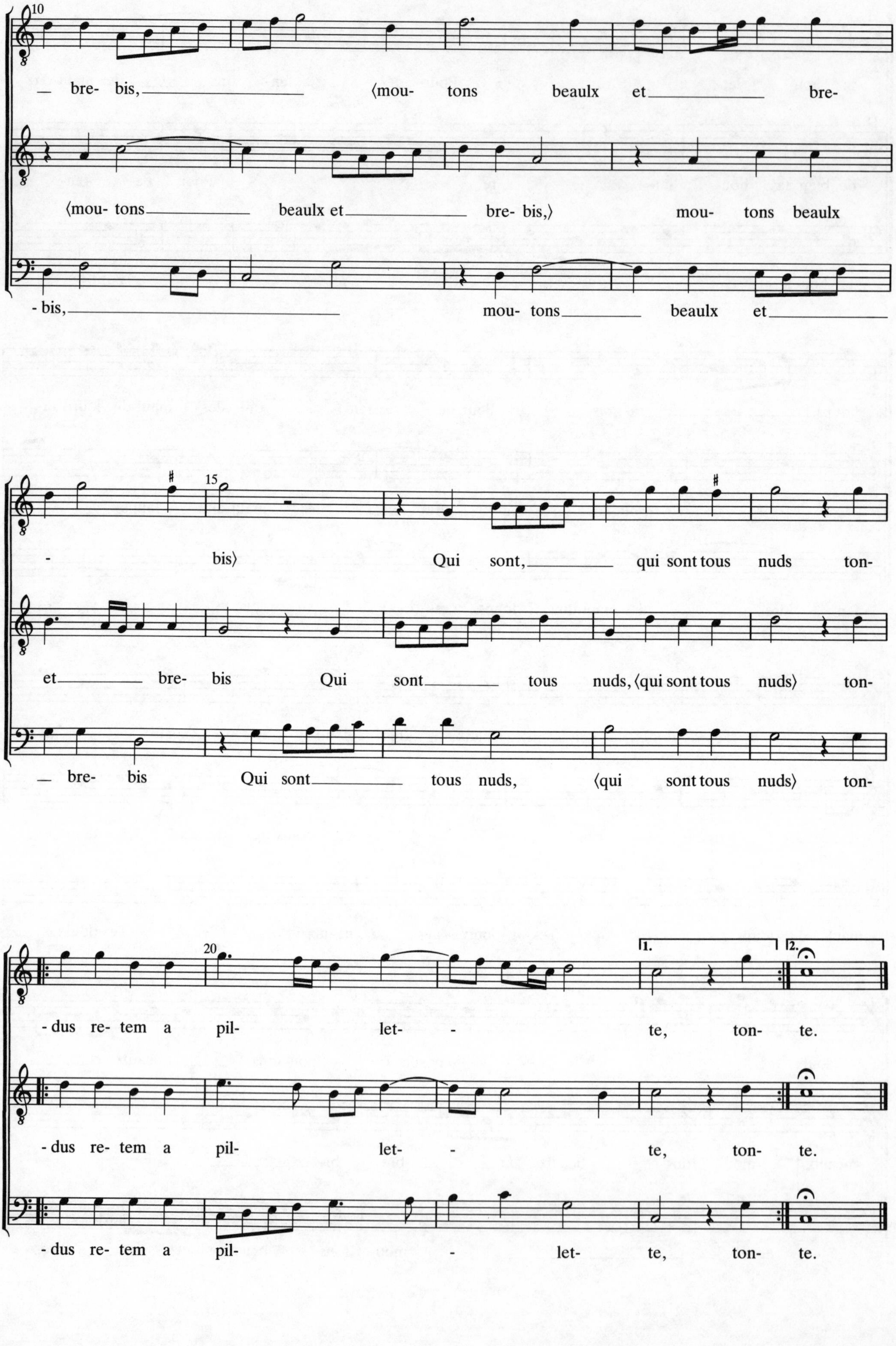
10
— bre- bis, ⟨mou- tons beaulx et bre-
⟨mou- tons beaulx et bre- bis,⟩ mou- tons beaulx
-bis, mou- tons beaulx et
15
- bis⟩ Qui sont, qui sont tous nuds ton-
et bre- bis Qui sont tous nuds, ⟨qui sont tous nuds⟩ ton-
— bre- bis Qui sont tous nuds, ⟨qui sont tous nuds⟩ ton-
20
1.
2.
-dus re- tem a pil- let- - te, ton- te.
-dus re- tem a pil- let- - te, ton- te.
-dus re- tem a pil- - let- te, ton- te.

# [21] La tres doulce plaisant velue

[Anonymous]

Cantus
La tres doul- ce plai- sant ve-
Tenor
La tres doul- ce plai- sant ve- lu-
Bassus
La tres doul- ce plai- sant ve- lu- - e,
5
- lu- - e, ve- lu- - e
- e, ve- lu- - e
ve- lu- - e, ⟨ve- - lu- e⟩ Sal-
10
Sal- lit l'au-trier en mi la ru- - e Pa-
Sal- lit l'au- trier en mi la ru- e
- lit l'au-trier en mi la ru- - e Pa- rée,

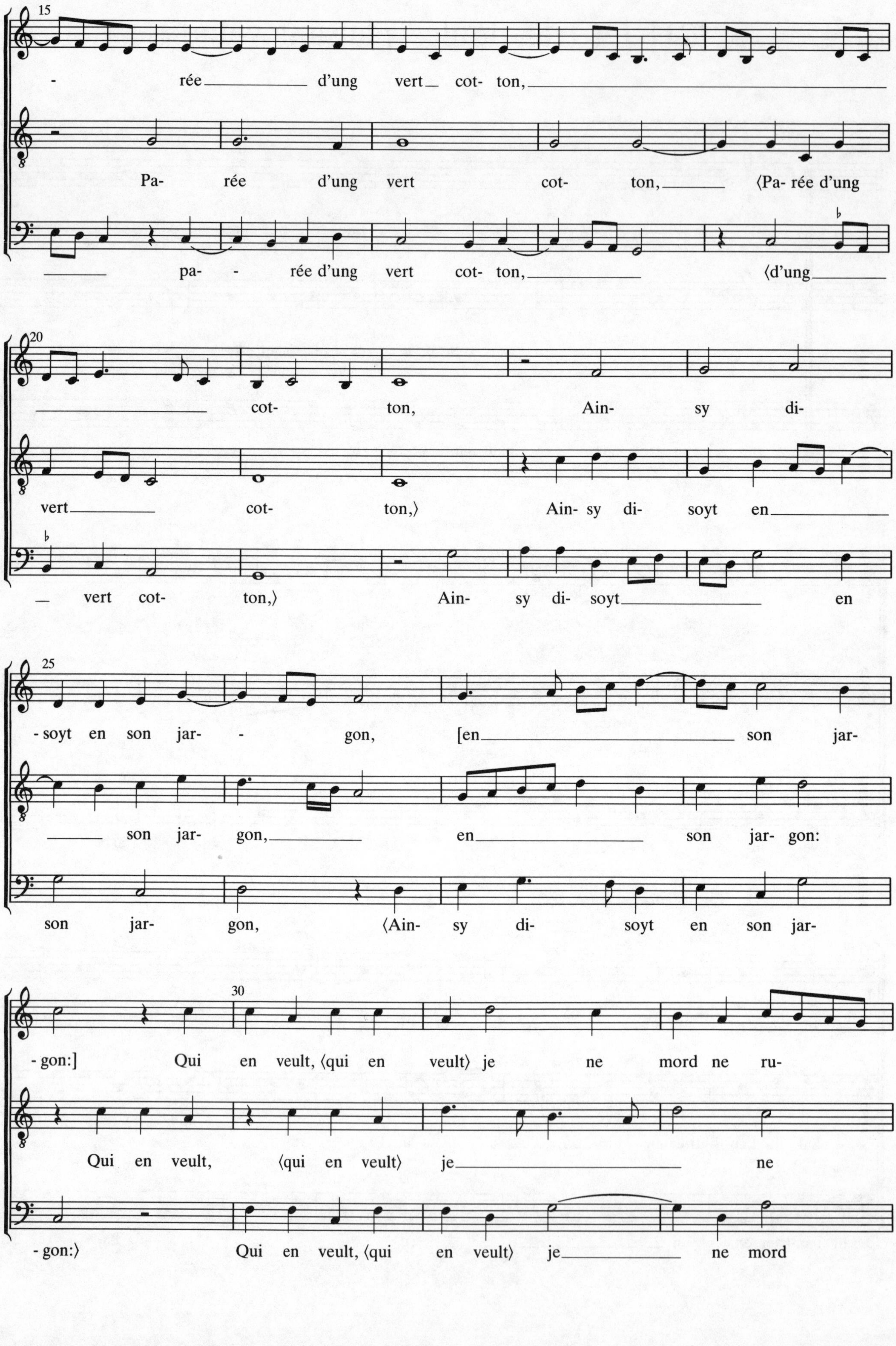
- rée d'ung vert cot- ton,
Pa- rée d'ung vert cot- ton, ⟨Pa- rée d'ung
pa- - rée d'ung vert cot- ton, ⟨d'ung
cot- ton, Ain- sy di-
vert cot- ton,⟩ Ain- sy di- soyt en
vert cot- ton,⟩ Ain- sy di- soyt en
- soyt en son jar- - gon, [en son jar-
son jar- gon, en son jar- gon:
son jar- gon, ⟨Ain- sy di- soyt en son jar-
- gon:] Qui en veult, ⟨qui en veult⟩ je ne mord ne ru-
Qui en veult, ⟨qui en veult⟩ je ne
- gon:⟩ Qui en veult, ⟨qui en veult⟩ je ne mord

35
- - e, Qui en veult, ⟨qui en
mord ne ru- e, Qui en veult, ⟨qui en veult⟩
ne ru- - - e, Qui en veult, ⟨qui
40
veult⟩ je ne mord ne ru- - - e.
je ne mord ne ru- e.
en veult⟩ je ne mord ne ru- - e.

# [22] Par fin despit je m'en iray seullette

[Claudin de Sermisy]

Cantus
Par fin des- pit je m'en i- ray seul- let-
Tenor
Par fin des- pit je m'en i- ray seul-
Bassus
Par fin des- pit je m'en i- ray seul- let-

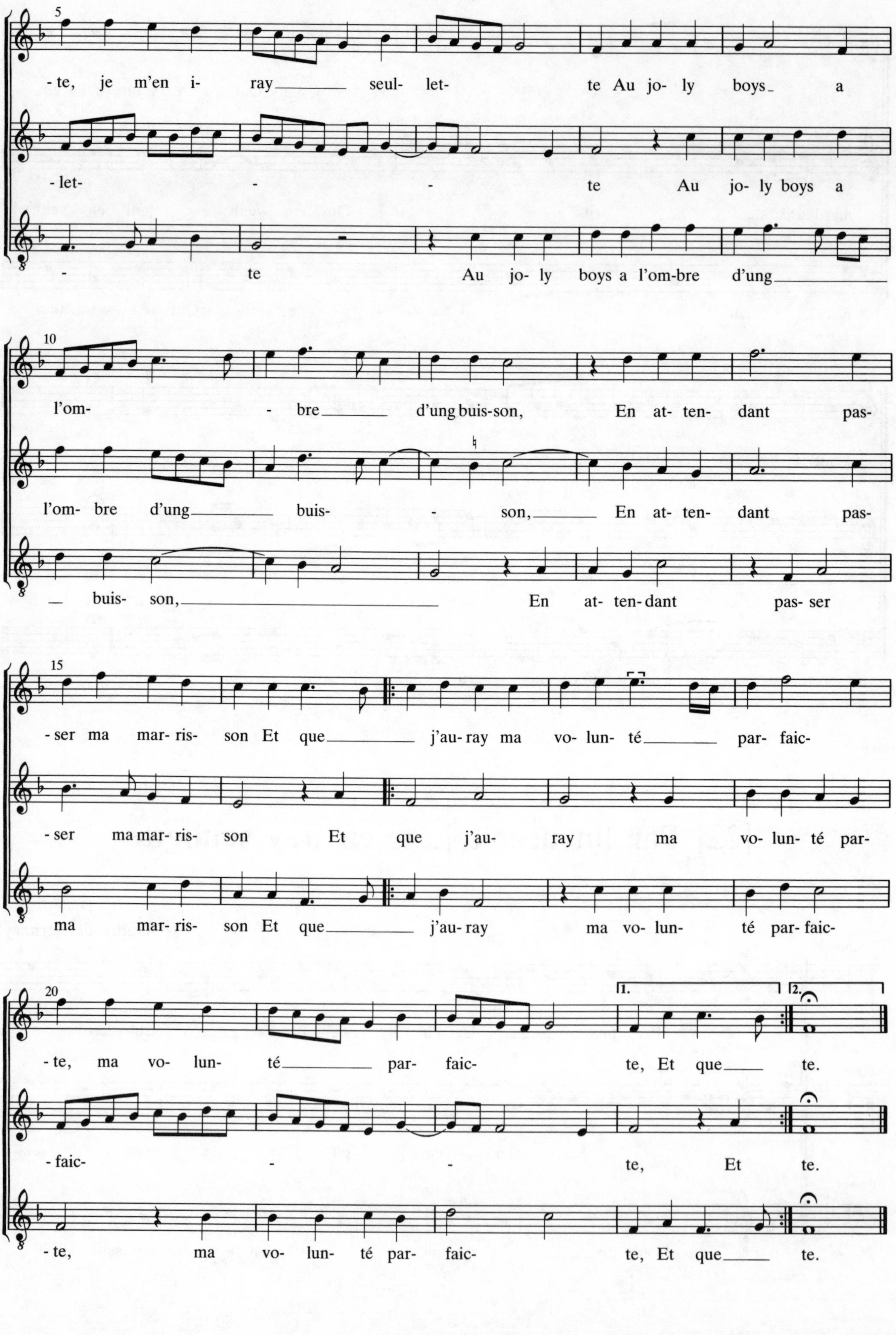
-te, je m'en i- ray seul- let- te Au jo- ly boys a
-let- - - te Au jo- ly boys a
- te Au jo- ly boys a l'om-bre d'ung
l'om- - bre d'ung buis-son, En at- ten- dant pas-
l'om- bre d'ung buis- - son, En at- ten- dant pas-
buis- son, En at- ten-dant pas- ser
-ser ma mar-ris- son Et que j'au- ray ma vo- lun- té par- faic-
-ser ma mar- ris- son Et que j'au- ray ma vo- lun- té par-
ma mar- ris- son Et que j'au- ray ma vo- lun- té par- faic-
-te, ma vo- lun- té par- faic- te, Et que te.
-faic- - - te, Et te.
-te, ma vo- lun- té par- faic- te, Et que te.

# [23] Si mon malheur my continue

[Claudin de Sermisy]

Cantus
Tenor
Bassus
Si mon mal- heur my con- ti- nu- -
Si mon mal-heur my con- - ti- nu-
Si mon mal-heur my con- ti- nu-
5
- - e, Je ne sçay pas, Je ne dis pas que je
- e, Je ne sçay pas, Je ne dis pas que je
- e, Je ne sçay pas, Je ne dis pas que je
10
fe- ray; A tout le moins je chan- - ge- ray Si le
fe- ray; A tout le moins je chan- - ge- ray Si
fe- ray; A tout le moins je chan- ge- ray
15
cou- rai- ge ne my mu- - e, Si le e.
le cou- rai- ge ne my mu- e, Si e.
Si le cou- rai- ge ne my mu- - e, e.
1.
2.

# [24] C'est malencontre que d'aymer

[Anonymous]

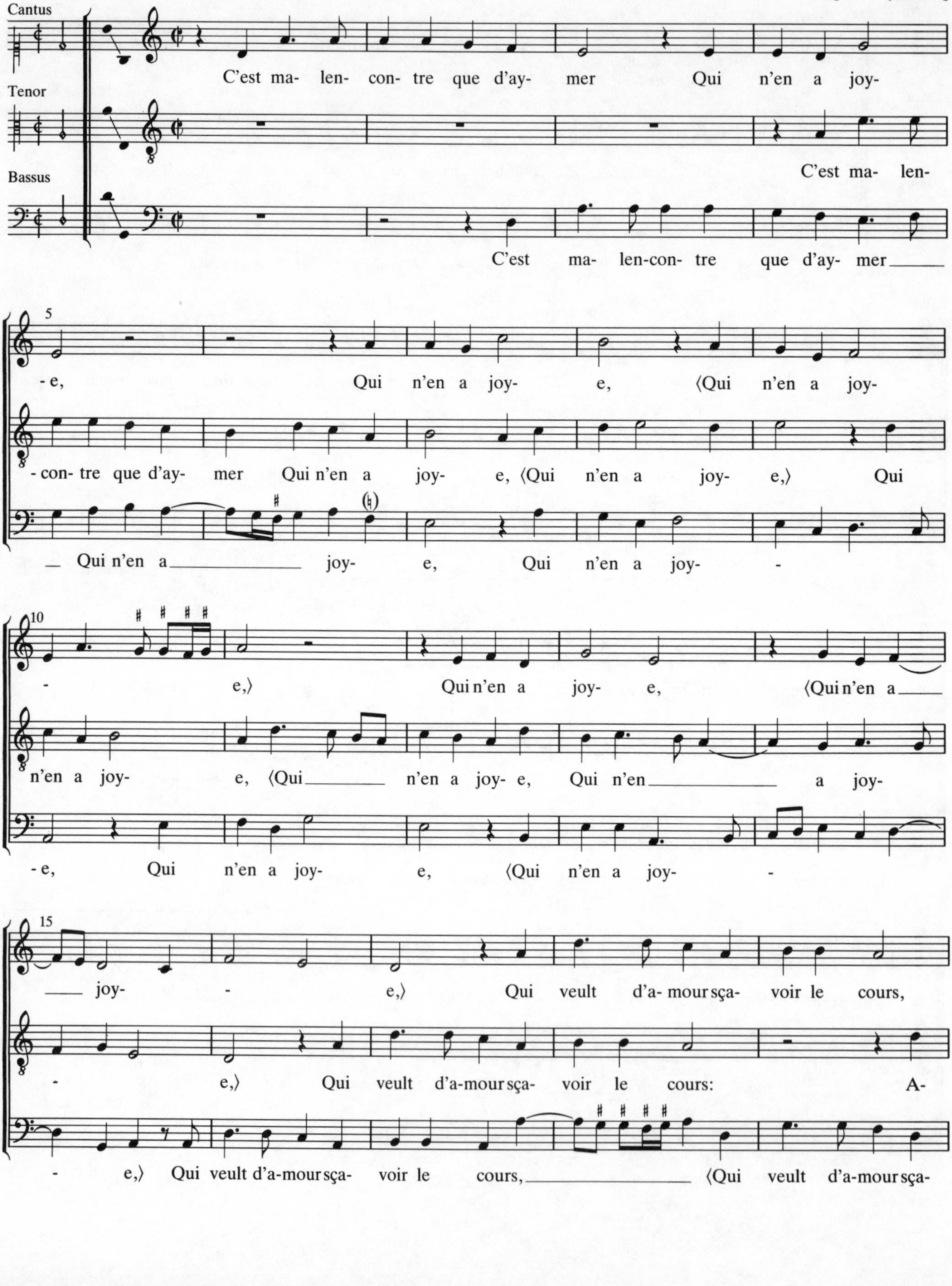

Cantus
Tenor
Bassus
C'est ma- len- con- tre que d'ay- mer Qui n'en a joy-
C'est ma- len-
C'est ma- len-con- tre que d'ay- mer
5
-e, Qui n'en a joy- e, ⟨Qui n'en a joy-
-con- tre que d'ay- mer Qui n'en a joy- e, ⟨Qui n'en a joy- e,⟩ Qui
Qui n'en a joy- e, Qui n'en a joy- -
10
- e,⟩ Qui n'en a joy- e, ⟨Qui n'en a
n'en a joy- e, ⟨Qui n'en a joy- e, Qui n'en a joy-
-e, Qui n'en a joy- e, ⟨Qui n'en a joy- -
15
joy- - e,⟩ Qui veult d'a-mour sça- voir le cours,
- e,⟩ Qui veult d'a-mour sça- voir le cours: A-
- e,⟩ Qui veult d'a-mour sça- voir le cours, ⟨Qui veult d'a-mour sça-

20
⟨Qui veult d'a-mour sça- voir le cours:⟩ A- mours font
- mours font fai- re [maints dé- tours,] A- mours font fai- re maints dé-
- voir le cours:⟩ A- mours font fai- re maints dé- tours,
25
fai- re maints dé- tours Et
- tours Et en- - gen-
⟨A-mours font fai- re maints dé- tours⟩ Et en- gen-drer cou- roux et plours,
30
en- gen-drer cou- roux et plours, [et plours] Donc je lar- moy-
- drer cou- roux et plours Donc
⟨cou- roux et plours⟩ Donc je lar- moy- - -
35
- e, ⟨Donc je lar- moy- - e⟩ Par
je lar- moy- e, Donc je lar- - moy- - e
- e, ⟨Donc je lar- moy- e,⟩ Donc je lar- moy-

40
ung qui-dam qui nuit et jour Si mi guer- - roy- e,
Par ung qui- - dam qui nuit et jour Si mi guer- roy- e,
- e Par ung qui- dam qui nuit et jour Si mi guer-roy-
45
Si mi guer- roy- - e. C'est ma- len-
— ⟨Par ung qui- dam qui nuit et jour Si mi guer-roy-
- e, ⟨Si mi guer- roy- -
50
- con- tre que d'ay- mer Qui n'en a joy- e, ⟨Qui
- e;⟩ C'est ma- len- con- tre que d'ay- mer Qui n'en a
- e,⟩ C'est ma- len-con- tre que d'ay- mer Qui n'en a joy-
55
n'en a joy- e,⟩ Qui n'en a joy- - e,
joy- e, ⟨Qui n'en a joy- e,⟩ Qui n'en a joy- e, ⟨Qui
- e, Qui n'en a joy- - e, ⟨Qui n'en a joy-

60
⟨Qui n'en a joy- e,⟩ Qui n'en a joy- e.
n'en a joy- e,⟩ [Qui n'en a joy- - e.]
- e,⟩ Qui n'en a joy- - - e.

# [25] En disant une chansonette

[Mathieu Gascongne]

Cantus
Tenor
Bassus
En di- sant u- - ne chan- so-
En di- sant u- ne chan- so- -
5
- net- te, ⟨En di- sant u- ne chan- - so- - net-
En di- sant u- - ne chan- so- - net-
- net- te, En di- sant u- ne chan- so- net-

-te⟩ Je vi- re u- ne da- me bru- net- te,
-te Je vi- re u- ne da- me bru- - net-
-te, Je vi- re u- ne da- me bru- net-
⟨Je vi- re u- ne da- me bru- net- - te,⟩ Je
- te, ⟨Je vi- re u- - ne da- me bru- net- - te,⟩
-te, ⟨Je vi- re u- ne da- me⟩ bru- net- - te, bru- - net- te,
vi- re u- ne da- me bru- - - net-
Al- la- quel- le pour al- ber- - ger, Al-
Je vi- re u- ne da- me bru- net- te, Al- la- quel-
-te, Al- la- quel- le pour
-la- quel- le pour al- ber- ger
-le pour al- ber- ger, Al- la- quel- le pour

al- ber- ger Je dis, me vo- lés vous lo-
Je dis, me vo- lés vous lo- ger En
al- ber- ger Je dis, me vo- lés vous lo-
- ger ⟨me vo- lés vous lo- - ger⟩
nuit en vos- tre mai- so- net- te, ⟨En nuit en vos- tre mai-
- ger, ⟨me vo- lés vous lo- ger⟩ En nuit en vos- tre mai- so-
En nuit en vos- - tre mai- so- net- - te,
- so- net- - te,⟩ en vos- - tre mai- so- net- te, mai-
- net- - te, en vos- tre mai- so- net-
mai- so- net- te?
- so- net- - te?
- te, en vos- tre mai- so- net- te?

# [26] Je suis trop jeunette

[Mathieu Gascongne or Nicolas Gombert]

Cantus
Je suis trop jeu- net- te Pour fai- re ung a-
Tenor
Je suis trop jeu- net- te Pour
Bassus
Je suis trop
5
-my, Pour fai- re ung a- my.
fai- re ung a- my, [ung a- my]. Si suis je
jeu- net- te Pour fai- re ung a- my. Si
10
Si suis je bien pres- te D'en fai-
bien pres- te D'en fai- - re ung jo- - ly, ⟨D'en
suis je bien pres- te, ⟨Si suis je bien pres- te⟩

15
-re͜ung jo- - ly, S'il est a ma pos- te,
fai- re͜ung jo- - ly,⟩ S'il est a ma pos- te, Il au-
D'en fai- - re͜ung jo- ly, S'il est a ma
20
⟨S'il est a ma pos- te,⟩ Il au- ra
-ra mon cueur, Il au- ra mon cueur, [mon
pos- te, Il au- ra mon cueur, ⟨Il au- ra
25
mon cueur. Je lay- ray mon pe- re, Ma me- - re,
cueur.] Je lay- ray mon pe- re, Ma
mon cueur.⟩ Je lay- ray mon pe- re, Ma me-
30
mon fre- - re, ma seur, M'en i- ray seu- let- te
me- re, mon fre- re, ma seur, M'en
- re, mon fre- re, ma seur, M'en i- ray seu- let- te Au boys a-

Au boys a- vec lui, Au boys a- - vec
i- ray seu- let- te Au boys a- vec lui, [a- vec
-vec lui, M'en i- ray seu- let- te Au boys a- vec lui
lui Cuil- lir vi- o- let- te
lui] Cuil- lir vi- - o- let- te Pour pas- - ser en-
Cuil- lir vi- o- let- te, ⟨Cuil- lir vi- o-
Pour pas- ser en- - nuy,
- nuy, ⟨Pour pas- ser en- nuy,⟩ Pour pas- ser en-
-let- te⟩ Pour pas- - ser en- nuy, ⟨Pour pas- ser
Pour pas- ser en- - - nuy.
- nuy, Pour pas- - ser en- nuy.
en- nuy,⟩ Pour pas- ser en- nuy.

# [27] J'ay contenté ma volunté suffisement

[Clément Marot] [Claudin de Sermisy]

Cantus
Tenor
Bassus
J'ay con- ten- té ma vo- lun- té suf- fi-
J'ay con- ten- té ma vo- lun- té suf- fi-
J'ay con- ten- té ma vo- lun- té suf- fi-
- se- ment Car j'ay es- té d'a- mours traic- té
- se- ment Car j'ay es- té d'a- mours traic- té di-
- se- ment
di- ver- se- ment. J'ay eu tour- ment,
- ver- se- ment, [di- ver- se- - ment.] J'ay eu
Car j'ay es- té d'a-mours traic- té di- ver- se- ment. J'ay
bon traic- - te- - - ment,
tour- ment, bon traic- te- ment, J'ay eu doul-
eu tour- ment, bon traic- te- ment, J'ay eu doul- ceur

20
J'ay eu doul- ceur et cru- -
- ceur et cru- - aul- -
et cru- aul- - té, [et cru-
[o = o·] 25
- aul- té, Et ne me plains fors seul- le-
- té, Et ne me plains fors seul- le- ment
- aul- té,] Et ne me plains fors seul- le-
30
[o· = o]
- ment D'a- voir ay- mé si loy- aul- ment Cel- le qui
D'a- voir ay- mé si loy- aul- ment Cel- le
- ment D'a- voir ay- mé si loy- aul- ment Cel-
35
est sans loy- - aul- - té, ⟨Cel- le qui
qui est sans loy- - aul- té, Cel- le
- le qui est sans loy- - aul- té, Cel- le

1.
2.
40
est sans loy- aul- - té,⟩ Cel- le qui - té.⟩
qui est sans loy- aul- té, Cel- le aul- té.
qui est sans loy- aul- té, Cel- aul- té.

# [28] C'est donc pour moy que ansins suis fortunée

[Ninot le Petit or Adrian Willaert]

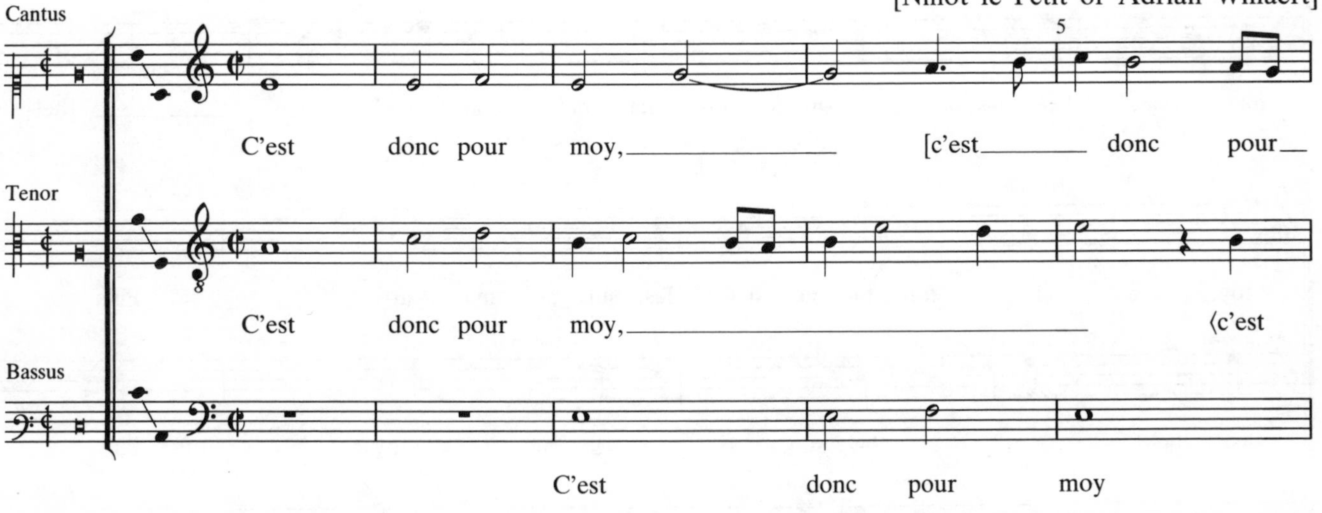
Cantus
Tenor
Bassus
5
C'est donc pour moy, [c'est donc pour
C'est donc pour moy, ⟨c'est
C'est donc pour moy

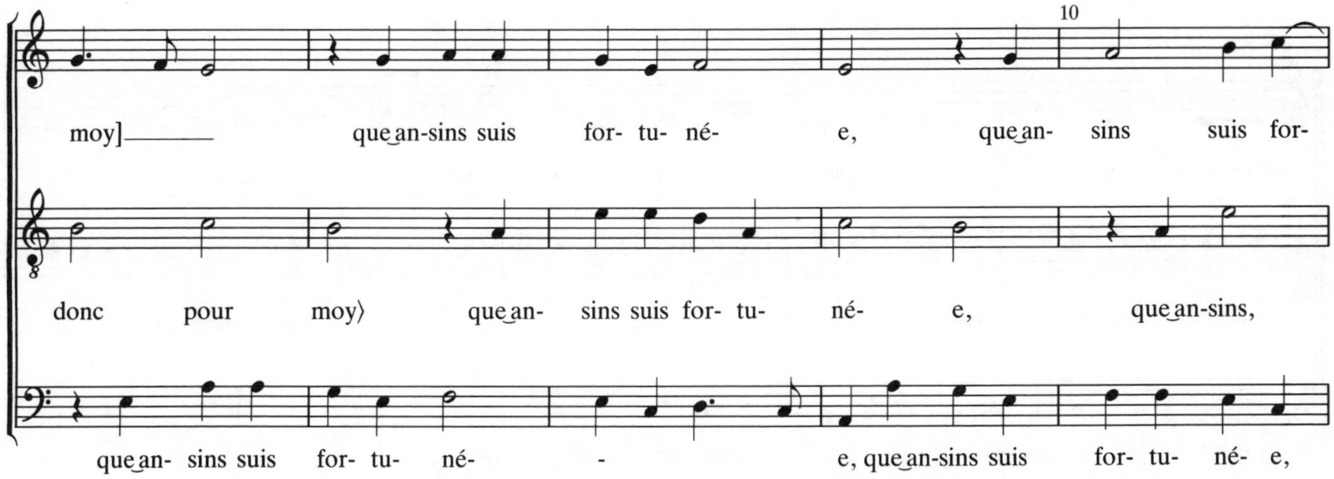
10
moy] que‿an-sins suis for- tu- né- e, que‿an- sins suis for-
donc pour moy⟩ que‿an- sins suis for- tu- né- e, que‿an-sins,
que‿an- sins suis for- tu- né- - e, que‿an-sins suis for- tu- né- e,

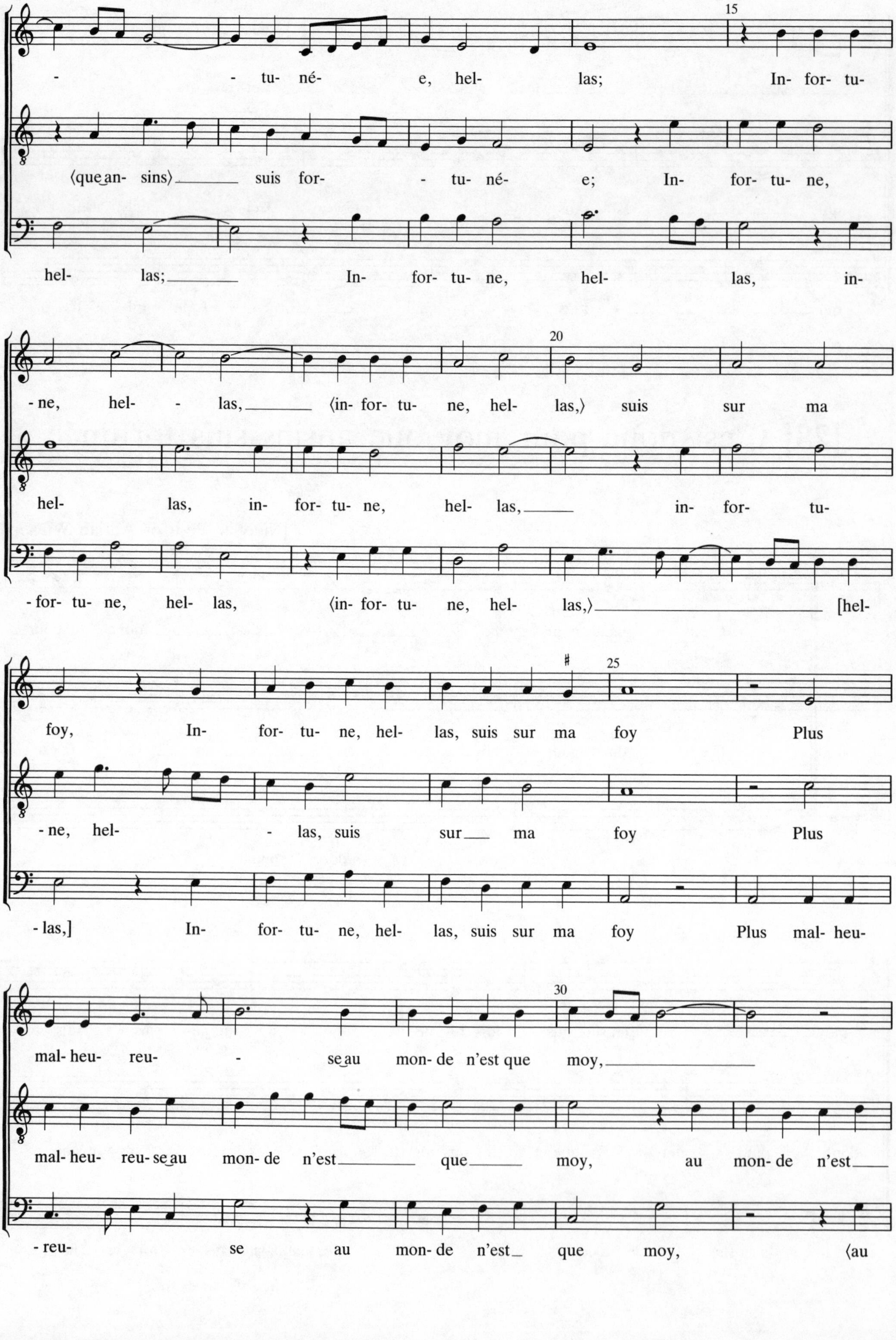
- - tu- né- e, hel- las; In- for- tu-
⟨que an- sins⟩ suis for- - tu- né- e; In- for- tu- ne,
hel- las; In- for- tu- ne, hel- las, in-
-ne, hel- - las, ⟨in- for- tu- ne, hel- las,⟩ suis sur ma
hel- las, in- for- tu- ne, hel- las, in- for- tu-
-for- tu- ne, hel- las, ⟨in- for- tu- ne, hel- las,⟩ [hel-
foy, In- for- tu- ne, hel- las, suis sur ma foy Plus
-ne, hel- - las, suis sur ma foy Plus
-las,] In- for- tu- ne, hel- las, suis sur ma foy Plus mal- heu-
mal- heu- reu- - se au mon- de n'est que moy,
mal- heu- reu- se au mon- de n'est que moy, au mon- de n'est
-reu- se au mon- de n'est que moy, ⟨au

au mon- de n'est que moy;
que moy, au mon- de n'est que moy;
mon- de n'est que moy,⟩ ⟨au mon- de n'est que moy;⟩
Aul- tre que moy, aul- tre que moy n'est de
Aul- tre que moy, aul- tre que moy n'est de
Aul- tre que moy, aul- tre que moy
tel- le heu- re né- e, Aul- tre que moy,
tel- le heu- re né- e, Aul- tre que moy,
n'est de tel- le heu- re né- e, Aul- tre que moy,
aul- tre que moy n'est de tel- le heu- re né- e.
aul- tre que moy n'est de tel- le heu- re né- e.
aul- tre que moy n'est de tel- le heu- re né- e.

# [29] Si j'ay eu du mal ou du bien

[Gosse or Guillaume Ysoré]

Cantus
Si j'ay eu du mal ou du bien Par
Tenor
Si j'ay eu du mal ou du bien Par ou- bli
Bassus
Si j'ay eu du mal ou du bien Par
5
ou- bli ou par sou- ve- nir, Je ne me veulx plain-dre
ou par sou- - ve- nir, Je ne me veulx plain-
ou- bli ou par sou- ve- nir, Je ne me veulx plain- dre de rien.
10
de rien. Dieu me doit mieulx a l'ad- ve- nir,
- dre de rien. Dieu me doit mieulx a l'ad- - ve-
Dieu me doit mieulx a l'ad- ve- nir,

Mais je vous prie de re- - te- nir
- nir, Mais je vous prie de re- te- nir De- sor- mais
Mais je vous prie de re- - te- nir De- sor- mais en
De- sor- mais en vos- tre pen- sé- - e
en vos- tre pen- sé- e Qu'a- mi- tyé qui se
vos- tre pen- sé- e
Qu'a- mi- tyé qui se peult fi- nir Ne
peult fi- nir Ne fut ja- - mais bien com- men-
Qu'a- mi- tyé qui se peult fi- nir Ne fut ja- mais bien
fut ja- mais bien com- men- cé- - e, e.
- cé- - e, Qu'a- mi- tyé qui se e.
com- men- cé- e, ⟨com- men- cé- e,⟩ e.

# [30] Changeons propos, c'est trop chanté d'amours

[Clément Marot] [Claudin de Sermisy]

Cantus
Chan- geons pro- pos, c'est trop chan-
Tenor
Chan- geons pro- pos, c'est trop chan- té
Bassus
Chan-geons pro- pos, c'est trop chan- té d'a- mours;
5
-té d'a-mours; Ce sont cla- mours, chan-tons de la ser- pet- -
d'a- mours; Ce sont cla- mours, chan-
Ce sont cla- mours, chan-tons de la ser- - pet- -
10
-te, de la ser- - pet- te. Tous vi- gne- rons
-tons de la ser- - pet- te. Tous vi- gne- rons ont a
-te, de la ser- pet- te. Tous vi- gne- rons ont a el- le re- cours,

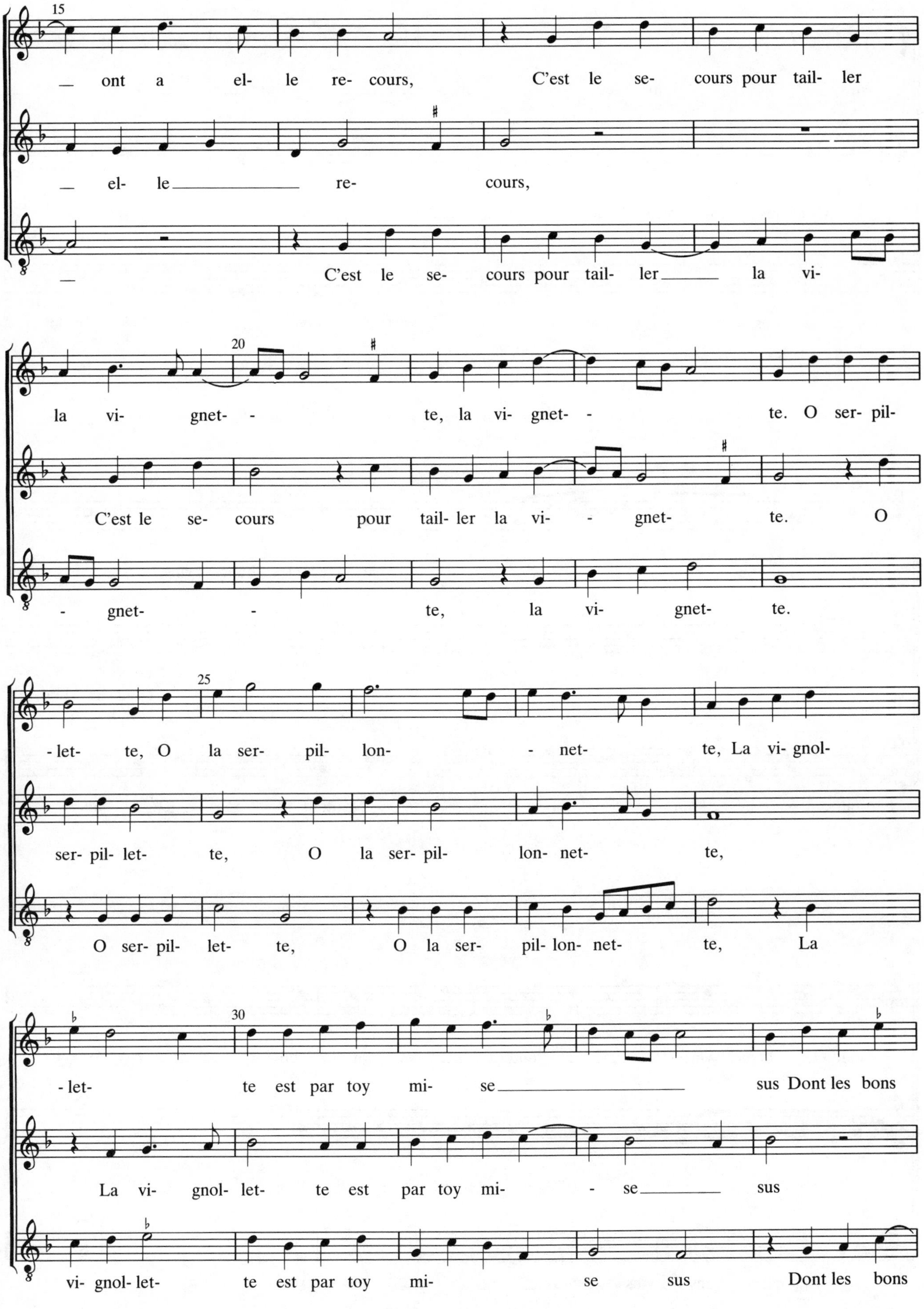
15
— ont a el- le re- cours, C'est le se- cours pour tail- ler
— el- le re- cours,
— C'est le se- cours pour tail- ler la vi-
20
la vi- gnet- - te, la vi- gnet- - te. O ser- pil-
C'est le se- cours pour tail- ler la vi- - gnet- te. O
- gnet- - te, la vi- gnet- te.
25
- let- te, O la ser- pil- lon- - net- te, La vi- gnol-
ser- pil- let- te, O la ser- pil- lon- net- te,
O ser- pil- let- te, O la ser- pil- lon- net- te, La
30
- let- te est par toy mi- se sus Dont les bons
La vi- gnol- let- te est par toy mi- - se sus
vi- gnol- let- te est par toy mi- se sus Dont les bons

vins, ⟨dont les bons vins⟩ tous les ans
Dont les bons vins tous les ans
vins, ⟨dont les bons vins⟩ tous les ans
sont ys- - sus, Dont les bons vins,
sont ys- - sus, Dont les bons
sont ys- sus, Dont les bons vins, ⟨dont les bons vins,⟩
⟨dont les bons vins⟩ tous les ans sont ys- sus.
vins tous les ans sont ys- sus.
dont les bons vins tous les ans sont ys- sus.